CYNTHIA MELTON

Kasdeya

The Fate of the Faes, Book 3

By Cynthia Melton

DEDICATION

To   all those who tirelessly fight the battle between
Good and Evil

Character List:

Faeries

Shayna
Deema
Queen Linette
Earin
Alvar

Humans

Pierce Cochran
Clark Payson
Luke Marshal
Chief-of-Police Rosen
Kasdeya (former demon follower)
Hanna
Logan
William Castion (mercenary leader)
Harry Dodge (SWAT team leader)

Other races

Abaddon – Leader of the dark
Radella – vampire
Seamus – Leprechaun
Paddy – Leprechaun
Gorna – dragon
Dragona - dragon
Agatha – witch
Rachel – witch
Lucille – witch

Lisa – witch
Becky – witch
Mary Ann - witch
Linc – Shifter – panther
Ennis – gnome
Olga - giant

1

Kasdeya

Kasdeya scrambled up a ladder in the subway to the street above and merged with the crowd. She couldn't be captured. Not yet. She had to live long enough to get revenge on Abaddon. A quick glance behind her showed Marshal quickly gaining. Before she'd been reverted to human form, before her injuries, she could have left the man far behind her. No longer. Now she was nothing more than a mere mortal, with all the setbacks that came with it.

"Just listen to me." Marshal raced after her.

"Help me." Kasdeya gripped the arm of a large man next to her. "Stop him. He'll hurt me."

While the stranger blocked Marshal's path, Kasdeya ducked into a corner café and out the back door. With a quick glance both ways, she chose right and sprinted down the alley, one arm pressed to her battered ribcage.

Coming back onto the busy New York street, she continued her flight. With no money and no food, her only option was a women's shelter a few blocks over. That or a church. She was pretty sure God wouldn't let her step one toe inside His house. Women's shelter it was.

She barged through the double doors and leaned against the wall, struggling to catch her breath against the pain in her side. A middle-aged woman rushed to help Kasdeya into a chair.

"Oh, dear." She snapped her fingers at a younger woman. "Get the doctor." She turned back to Kasdeya. "Who hurt you, honey? Do you want me to call the police? What's your name?"

Too many questions. "No police, thank you. The man who…mugged me is long gone. My name is Kassy."

"Come on, let's get you taken care of, fed, and cleaned up." She helped Kasdeya to a back room and handed her a towel. "Shower is right through there. Just wrap the towel around you so the doctor can get a good look at your injuries. I'll be right here if you need me. Are you hungry?"

Kasdeya nodded on her way to the shower. She stripped down and laid her red leather jacket and pants on a nearby stool. They'd need cleaning but would have to go to a dry cleaner. She could change into something else, but the leather made her feel fierce, and she'd worn it for a very long time. So long it had become like a second skin to her.

Closing her eyes, she stepped under the hot spray of the shower and let the water wash away the grime from the tunnels and ease some of the aching from her shoulders. Tears rolled down her cheeks, disappearing down the drain with the water. If only she'd killed the child. Then, she'd still be Abaddon's right hand and powerful. Her heart wasn't as dark as people believed after all.

After her shower, a strange woman waited in the next room. "I'm Doctor Clark. Sit on this cot and let me take a look at you. Doris brought you a dress."

"I'd like to wear the red." Kasdeya sat, turning a suspicious gaze on the doctor. Learning to trust humans again would take some time.

"Let's at least get it cleaned, shall we?" The doctor listened to her heart, her lungs, then had her lie back so she could gently press her ribcage. "I suspect you have some fractures but no hard breaks. That is good. I'll wrap you up and tend to your scrapes. Would you like to tell me what happened?"

"I betrayed a powerful man."

The doctor made a disgusted sound in her throat. "That will get you beat up every time. My advice to you is to stay away from him."

Kasdeya nodded, intending anything but staying away. Once she found a way to destroy the leader of the dead, she'd make sure he joined those who blindly followed him into hell. When the doctor left, giving her something for the pain, Kasdeya donned the simple red and yellow sundress, then lay back and fell asleep.

Marshal

Where could she have gone? Marshal stood on the street corner, hands on his hips, and glared at the big brute who'd stopped him. "I ought to arrest you for obstruction of justice."

The man held up his hands. "I had no idea you were a cop." The grin on his face and the tone of his voice sounded as if it wouldn't have mattered. His actions would have been the same if he'd known Marshal was law enforcement.

Marshal groaned. In a city the size of New York, a city where the sky darkened with each day and undead roamed the streets, Kasdeya could be anywhere. "Get inside, dude. Haven't you heard? It's not safe on the streets anymore."

"Yeah, I heard about the vampires. Crazy stuff, but my kids got to eat." He shook his head and strolled away, slapping a hard hat on.

The man worked outside? He'd be joining the undead before the week was out if he didn't stay extra-vigilant. Marshal shoved his hands in his pockets and hurried to the portal.

Reconstruction from the traitor Alvar's attack was in full force on rebuilding the palace despite Queen Shayna's insistence that she'd rather rule her people under the sky and trees than in a marble palace, no matter how grand the building.

He located her on a makeshift throne placed under the drooping branches of a willow tree. At her side sat Pierce. The clang of swords proved Deema and Payson were hard at work on the training field. After the death of many warriors, new ones needed to be brought up for the approaching battle.

"No Kasdeya?" Shayna frowned.

"She convinced some brute of a man to step in front of me. By the time I got around him, she had disappeared. I'll head out again at dark." Not that the day wasn't already as dark as dusk.

He accepted a crystal goblet of water from a passing steward. "Before you say no, I understand the danger, but if she comes out of hiding, it will be under the cover of darkness. I've got my necklace." He pulled the cross from under his shirt. "My bottle of holy water and my sword. I'll be fine. I have a better chance of getting her to listen if I'm alone. If we approach her as a group, she'll see it as a sign of force and keep running."

"I still think she can't be trusted." Deema stopped next to them.

"I believe everyone should get a second chance." Shayna leaned forward. "Once she's caught, she is your responsibility, Marshal. You cannot let her betray us. Once she crosses the portal, she must be kept on a tight rein until her faithfulness is proven. The fact that she didn't kill Hanna is not enough proof for me that she is willing to change."

"I understand." His heart told him the former demon follower was no longer the same person, but his head agreed with Deema. He'd have to be careful. "How is Rachel's boy coming along in his training?"

Deema grinned. "With the same potion Agatha gave you three detectives, he's coming along surprisingly well. The young man is like a dancer on the battlefield. Yes, Logan will be an asset in a fight, even at the young age of fifteen." Her smile faded. "I'd like to say Kasdeya can't be changed, but I came back to the Light. If she proves her loyalty, I'll fight by her side." With those words, the faerie marched away.

He turned back to Shayna. "I just want her to have a chance."

"She will have one, but only one chance." Shayna smiled. "Go get some rest and eat. Go in the Light, Marshal. You've a good heart."

Maybe, but it hadn't always been that way. When he'd first found out that faeries, demons, and the like existed outside the pages of a fairy tale, he'd been more than skeptical. He'd been angry and disillusioned at the rising crime and death rate in a world he loved. Now, having encountered demons and vampires face-to-face, gratitude to fight on the side of the Light filled him. At least the side he fought for had hope.

He sat at the end of a long table next to the training grounds and ate with the warriors. No matter how much Shayna called him one, he could never see himself as one of them. The faeries were ferocious in battle and fought without fear. Every time he lifted his sword, his knees almost buckled under the weight of his own fear. Still, they accepted him now as one of their own and welcomed him as he took his seat.

"I can send a fighter or two to help you in your search," Earin said, passing a plate of something blue.

Marshal had never tasted anything as good as

what was served in The Glen, nor any food as brightly colored. "No, I'd best do this alone, but thanks." He finished eating, showered under the waterfall, and ducked back through the portal.

If he were a wounded, frightened woman who felt she had no one to trust, where would he go? He scoured the churches around the area he'd last seen Kasdeya, but no one had seen her. He hit pay dirt on the second women's shelter he located because the gray-haired general at the door would not allow him in.

"I'm a detective. I need to locate this woman for her own protection." He showed his badge.

"Unless she's broken the law and you intend to arrest her, she is safer here." The woman crossed her arms.

They entered into a stare down. "I'll be back tomorrow with a warrant."

Alvar

Alvar rubbed his hands together. Getting rid of Kasdeya by convincing Abaddon she'd betray him over time was the best, most diabolical thing he'd ever done. Now he was the demon leader's right hand, not some human given immortality. A magical fae could do so much more in ridding the world of light.

He glanced to where Linc, the panther shapeshifter, lounged in front of a fire. The dark-skinned man, even in human form, seemed more like a cat than a man. "I need you to sniff her out," Alvar said. "Kasdeya must be destroyed. She knows too much." He ran his hand over the crystal ball he'd found near the old portal to The Glen. Little information came through, but he knew The Glen's occupants were rebuilding and training. If they recruited Kasdeya, things would veer in their favor.

"I'll go later," Linc said. "It's cold outside."

"Put on a jacket. Where's Radella?"

"I'm not her keeper." The man even had the temperament of a cat. If not for the luxury Alvar provided, the shifter would have no loyalty at all.

"I'm here." The beautiful vampire sashayed toward him and perched on the arm of the chair, handing him a whiskey and running her fingers through his hair. "What does my lord command?"

"My whiskey, then you in the bedroom, in that order." He smiled up at her. Since he'd freed her from the chains of The Glen's dungeon, she'd vowed undying loyalty and promised herself in return. Still, in bed, Alvar ordered her to wear a mouthpiece over her fangs. He might enjoy the vampire, but he didn't trust her not to bite during the throes of passion. She'd mentioned more than once she'd like to turn him.

He laughed. Power! The grandness of it. He had a powerful cat at his feet and a beautiful immortal woman on his arm. What more could a faerie ask for?

2

Kasdeya

Marshal had found her? Her blood raced as she changed into her red leather. She had to go. He couldn't find her, and she knew enough about the detective to know he'd be back.

"You need more rest," Doris said, shaking her head. "One more night."

"No. I have to go. Thank you for your help."

"Then take this." The woman thrust a drawstring bag into her hand. "It's got a little money, food, water, a blanket, and this dress." She shoved it inside. "Go in peace, Kassy."

Kasdeya forced a smile. She didn't deserve the woman's kindness. She didn't deserve life, for that matter, and would welcome death after Abaddon and Alvar were destroyed. "Thank you." She had money, though. Lots of it. Accessing the treasure was the problem. One that needed to be solved as soon as possible.

Ducking out the back door, she counted the money in the bag. A hundred dollars. Enough to get her to her family's estate. After her pledge of loyalty to Abaddon, she'd taken her millions out of the bank and buried it deep in the family cemetery. She hadn't needed it while following Abaddon. He'd seen to her every need.

She hailed a cab and settled back for the hour drive into the Adirondack mountains. The driver shrugged when she asked him to wait, promising she'd pay him for however long it took. Hitching the bag over her shoulder, she headed into the thick trees.

The cemetery looked like something out of a horror film with lichen and moss covering the gravestones. With her family gone, no one was left to maintain the family plots.

Ignoring the dead, she headed straight for the crypt on the opposite side. The door creaked as she forced it open and headed for the place where her great-great grandmother should have lain. Instead, the coffin held cash, stocks, bonds, and gold coins. Her grandmother lay in an unmarked plot somewhere else.

There was too much to be carried in one trip. Kasdeya stuffed the drawstring bag with hundred-dollar bills and slid the coffin back in place. She laid a hand on the carved wood. "Thank you." Feeling slightly better about her security, she hurried back to the cab.

He narrowed his eyes at her and turned off the radio. "Where to?"

"The Ritz." She handed him two of the bills.

"Wow, lady. Thanks." He folded the bills and put them in his pocket before pulling away from the road's shoulder and turning around.

The room she checked into made her feel right at home. The penthouse she'd once lived in still held the top spot for luxury, but this room would do nicely. She tossed the bag on the bed and went in search of the safe, locating it in a corner of the closet. After storing the money, she ordered room service and settled back with a bottle of wine from the in-room bar.

The knock of room service at the door woke her. She pushed to her feet, her ribs in protest, and peered through the peephole. An old man in a white jacket stared at the hole. Kasdeya opened the door and stepped back, ready to slam the door on his arm if he wasn't who he claimed to be.

"Anything else, ma'am?" He lifted his chin.

"If I give you a hundred dollars for the errand, will you purchase me a gun and a military-grade knife? Both red." She grinned. "I'd need you to be discreet. Hold them until morning. I will be sleeping soon and do not want to be awakened."

"Of course." Surprise flickered in his eyes.

"Good." She retrieved fifteen-hundred dollars from the safe. "Something that would fit my hand well and no more than fourteen-hundred dollars total. I'll want to see the receipt."

He nodded, took the money, and backed from the room.

"Oh, wait," she said, before closing the door. "Get me a silver cross necklace—real silver, and a vial of holy water.”

“Holy water?”

“Yes. Make sure it comes from a church. It has to be blessed.” She closed the door against his surprised expression and laughed. She’d be ready for whatever Alvar sent her way.

After eating the steak and baked potato she’d ordered, she glanced out the large window. Being on the twelfth floor gave her a prime view of the mostly deserted street below. Those who were brave enough to be out hurried from one destination to the next, staying close to the buildings in case they had to dart inside away from harm.

No longer did Kasdeya have a magic eye allowing her to see where the demons flew or the vampires lurked. Nor could she spot any faeries around. She was as blind as any other human who didn’t have their eyes opened by Shayna. As if the queen of The Glen would bestow such a favor on one who had sent the undead to kill her. She let the curtains fall into place, undressed, and stretched out on the comfortable bed. The Ritz would be the perfect place to hide and heal.

Marshal

“Found your girl.” When Marshal entered the precinct the next morning, Officer Charges waved a slip of paper at him. “A cab driver recognized your description on the radio. Says he dropped her at the

Ritz yesterday afternoon."

"That's good luck." Marshal snatched the paper from the man and headed to the hotel where he hoped Kasdeya would still be. He had a warrant for the women's shelter in his pocket but hoped the hotel would see it as enough evidence to let him in. If he had to arrest Kasdeya for her to go with him, he would.

The young girl at the front desk had no trouble telling him what room the woman in red rented. He leaned over the counter and glanced at the computer. Cassandra Brown? Close enough. "Thanks." He tossed her a wink and stepped into the elevator with a bellhop.

The man held a box with 1213 scribbled across the front.

"I'll deliver that for you." Marshal grabbed the box, showed his badge, and proceeded to ignore the man's nervous stammerings.

"The money she owes me is in that box."

Marshal opened the box. "A gun and a knife." Not to mention a silver cross and a vial of water. "Impressive." Two one-hundred-dollar bills and some loose change were stuffed between the two weapons. Marshal grabbed the cash and handed it to the bellhop. "I think this is your floor." He pressed the button to stop on floor five. "Keep the change."

"She said one hundred, and she's scary enough to make me only want that amount." He tried to hand one of the bills back.

"I'll tell her I said you could have it." Where had she gotten the money anyway? "Oh, I need your jacket."

He grinned at the startled man as he handed over his white jacket. The doors closed, and Marshal finished the ride to the twelfth floor. After donning the white jacket over his suit, he stepped from the elevator. He knocked on the door of room 1213 and turned around so Kasdeya couldn't see his face through the peep hole.

"You're late." The door behind him opened.

"You didn't make it easy." He whirled and forced himself inside. With his foot, he slammed the door behind him. "A gun and knife? I do hope you weren't going to use them on me."

Her chocolate-brown eyes narrowed. "Hand me the box and I will."

"Oh, and I gave two-hundred dollars to the bellhop. I knew you wouldn't mind." He reached behind him and locked the door.

Her shoulders slumped, and tears welled in her eyes. "You cannot kill me. I have to destroy Abaddon first."

"That's why I'm here, actually. The side of the Light needs your help in accomplishing that very thing." Man, he hated when women cried. Even women who had been a pain in his ass.

She shook her head. "Shayna will never forgive me."

"You're wrong. She may be the ruler, but she's also kind and fair. She'll listen before passing judgment." He held out his hand. "Trust me."

Their gazes locked for several seconds before she sighed. "All right. It isn't as if I have a choice. Wait here." She left the room.

He followed. "Not a chance. I go where you go.

It's kind of my job now."

"You're my watchdog?" Her eyes widened.

"Pretty much." He grinned and watched while she emptied the room safe. "You've been invited to The Glen."

She shuddered. "I'll be struck by lightning first thing."

"No, you won't." He laughed. "Come on. I'll hand this box to you when the time comes."

He'd never known a woman could stay silent as long as she did as they made their way to the portal, which would need to be changed again, and then into The Glen. Faeries scowled and shrank away as they passed.

Kasdeya squared her shoulders and kept walking, not glancing to the left or the right. When Marshal made his first time through, everything came at such a speed, he couldn't take it all in. Especially the pretty females in their semi-transparent gowns.

He led her to where Shayna strolled along a crushed shell path among bushes vibrant with flowers in every hue of the rainbow. She turned as they approached and motioned her head to a stone bench.

"Sit here, please," Marshal told Kasdeya.

She lowered herself slowly onto the seat, her gaze locked on Shayna's. The queen sat across from her. "Welcome to The Glen."

"Should I kneel?" Kasdeya turned to Marshal.

"I am not your queen," Shayna said. "But I do ask that you give me your full attention."

Kasdeya whirled back to face her as if she'd

been stung. "Or you'll kill me?"

Shayna's lips twitched. "Not unless I have to."

"I'll do my best to stay your hand." Kasdeya crossed her arms.

"Can the two of you act as if you aren't mortal enemies?" Marshal asked. "At least for today?"

"I will if she will." Kasdeya glared.

Shayna laughed and waved Pierce, who strolled toward them, forward. "Marshal has succeeded."

Pierce sat beside Shayna and focused on Kasdeya. "You look ill."

"I've some cracked ribs from a beating Abaddon gave me." Kasdeya glanced at the ground.

"Darling." Shayna put a hand on his arm. "Please fetch Nurse Ida. She can heal this woman."

He started to protest but caught Marshal's warning glance. He sighed and hurried away.

Rachel darted past him, the other four witches close behind her. She lifted her hand and blasted Kasdeya off the bench and into the bushes.

Shayna lunged to her feet.

Hanna threw herself in front of her mother. "Stop."

"Get out of my way, child."

"Mother, please. She saved my life." Hanna turned and helped Kasdeya to her feet.

"You will not do that here," Shayna said, her eyes hardening. "We've invited this woman into our midst. If discipline is required, I will be the one to do it."

"She took my child."

"And saved her life." Marshal moved next to Hanna providing a two-person shield in front of

Kasdeya. "She deserves to be heard. If you cannot stay quiet, you must go back to the tower."

Agatha put a hand on Rachel's arm. "Shayna will not do anything to jeopardize any of us here. She is queen." She ushered the women away.

The tension in Marshal's body relaxed as some of the anger left Rachel's face, and she lowered her hands. He helped Kasdeya back to sitting. "Are you okay?"

She nodded, although her breathing said otherwise.

"I think your ribs are more than cracked now." He glanced up as the nurse hurried toward them.

"Drink this." She held out a silver goblet.

"What is it?"

"It will heal you from more than the broken bones and bruises." The nurse smiled. "If you've any evil left in you, you'll die after two swallows."

Kasdeya tilted the glass and downed it, not stopping for air until it was empty.

3

Kasdeya

The drink tasted vile. Kasdeya drank and gagged, forcing the liquid to stay in her stomach. When she didn't die immediately, she grinned. "Looks like I passed that particular test."

Deema, who had joined them on the heels of the nurse, snarled. "You've more than just this test to pass."

Kasdeya shuddered. "I'll withstand anything you throw at me."

Shayna held up a hand to stop their squabbling. "Before I question you, I'd like to hear your story. Who you were before, why you became a follower of Abaddon…all of it. Will you share?"

Taking a deep breath, knowing refusal to answer would be seen as a sign of disloyalty, she nodded. "It isn't a pretty tale. I was born in 1879 as Cassandra Brown. A wealthy socialite, spoiled-rotten brat of a twit who didn't think society's rules applied to her." She twisted her hands in her lap. "When I turned twenty-one, I got involved with a man of the cloth and had a child out of wedlock. He tossed me aside, and my family disowned me…Abaddon found me in a brothel and offered me eternity and power. I never looked upon my child's face, and she'd be long dead by now." She locked gazes with Shayna. "I didn't think twice about accepting his offer. He stripped me of my humanity and gave me dominion over his demons. To a woman who had lost everything, that meant a lot."

Her gaze flicked to Marshal. The man looked as shocked as if he'd just heard his mother had been a prostitute in her younger days. "I'm one-hundred-and thirty-nine years old, but here in your time, my age is still twenty-one." Although she knew she looked ten years older. A hard life did that to a person.

"Why did Abaddon throw you out?" Shayna straightened. "You cannot lie in this place, no matter how hard you try."

"I've no need to lie." Kasdeya's shoulders rounded. "I don't know exactly, but I assume Alvar had something to do with my dismissal."

Shayna's face remained impassive as she thought. "Alvar seems to be declining in health and strength. How is he?"

She shrugged. "I don't know. We haven't seen each other for quite a while. He's been busy creating his monsters." Just his name left a sour taste in her mouth that had nothing to do with the potion she'd drunk.

"How can you help us? You're a human now. Mortal and without magic."

"I know Alvar's secrets. I want nothing more than to destroy Abaddon."

"Can he be destroyed? We thought him only capable of being held in chains."

Kasdeya's heart sank. "I hoped you'd know more than I." She squared her shoulders, surprised to find that her ribs no longer ached. "Use me as bait. I don't care how he's brought down, only that he is."

"Revenge is a poison that harms the one seeking the revenge more than the person you want to harm." Shayna narrowed her eyes. "We've no demons to test you with since Alvar released them. How can we prove you are truly willing to help us?"

"You've already given me a watchdog." She cut a sideways glance at Marshal. "I didn't kill the girl. What more would you ask?"

"You didn't raise a murderous hand to anyone, yet you were responsible for many deaths. You are not innocent, Kasdeya," Shayna's tone chilled.

"No one knows that more than I." Her throat clogged with tears. She glanced around the garden. A beautiful but strange place to hold an interrogation. In the distance, faeries worked like bees rebuilding a large marble structure. "Alvar destroyed your palace, killed your queen, released Radella and the demon, yet you sit here and question me relentlessly. Wouldn't our time be better spent making plans?"

"It would, but you must prove yourself first."

Shayna stood. "Marshal, put her in the tower with the witches, then find me." Head high, she strolled away, looking every bit the queen she now was.

"Come on." Marshal took her by the elbow.

"I really don't want to go with the witches." Hanna's mother would rather kill her than breathe the same air. "They scare me."

"Shayna said, so we do." He marched her to a tower that had withstood the wrath of Alvar.

A winding marble staircase led them upward ten stories. Once at the top, they stepped into a round room, and five pairs of eyes glared at them.

"What is she doing here?" Rachel's lip curled.

"Waiting for whatever may come." Kasdeya plopped into a nearby chair.

Marshal

A one-hundred-and-thirty-five-year-old socialite prostitute. Marshal rubbed his hands up and down his face, his palms rasping against the day's growth of stubble. It made it a little easier to understand how Abaddon had lured her to his side, but it was still a lot for a man to swallow.

From the serious, yet worried expression on Kasdeya's face, she knew the thoughts whirling through his head. He tried to give her a reassuring smile and failed. Throwing the lock on the door to slow Kasdeya down, should she choose to try and make a run for it, he moved to Agatha's side. "What are you working on?”

"A way to keep track of her," she said, motioning her head toward Kasdeya, "and making sure that any move toward helping the other side results in her immediate death. It's the only assurance we have that she won't betray us."

"You can make something like that?" He frowned.

"We're trying to. It will be something we implant under her skin." She held up a small silver disc. "Like a tracker, kind of."

"You people don't make second chances easy, do you?"

"Not when it could mean our lives, we don't." She dropped the disc into a smoking bowl, whispered an incantation over it, then moved to the other side of the table. The other women had already returned to grinding herbs at a sink.

"Now what are you doing?"

"Trying to come up with a way to keep us from being annihilated when we meet Alvar on that mountain range in Wyoming. Go away. I'm working."

He laughed and patted her back. The ancient witch was as crusty as bread left under the table and forgotten. Still, her skill with magic was indispensable. If she wanted to be left alone, then that was what he'd do. He moved to the window and gazed out upon the training field.

Kasdeya joined him. "I need to learn to fight."

He cut her a quick glance. "I assumed you already knew."

"Nope. Never held a sword in my life. I'm a

good shot with a gun, though, thanks to my father. Will that be of any help?"

"Maybe, with the right bullets." She'd also need armor, and he wasn't sure they could find a dragon willing to give up any scales for a former enemy.

A knock sounded on the door. He opened it to see Deema waiting. "Shayna is ready. Agatha?"

"Got it." The old woman retrieved the silver disc from the bowl and a hypodermic needle bigger than any Marshal had seen before.

The four trooped to the dining hall where a chair sat in the center of the floor, facing a line of other chairs. Marshal had Kasdeya sit in the single chair as Shayna and the others filed into the room.

Kasdeya's white-knuckled grip on the seat of the chair spoke volumes of what she felt, staring up at them as they sat across from her. "What's going to happen?"

"Well, dear, I'm going to give you a shot. Hold still." Agatha jabbed the needle into the upper part of Kasdeya's arm.

"Ow!" She whirled. "That was rougher than it needed to be. You could have at least let me take off my jacket rather than put a hole in it."

Agatha waved her hand, closing the hole in the leather. "Such a baby." She moved to stand behind Shayna.

Marshal bit his tongue in order not to say what was really on his mind. Kasdeya had come with him, somewhat willingly, and didn't deserve harsh treatment just because the others didn't like her.

Shayna shook her head. "Be nice, Agatha. My apologies, Kasdeya, but you must realize it will take some time for everyone to get over the past. We've implemented a tracker, more like a bomb, into your arm. We will know where you are at all times, but if your heart should once again side with the dark, it will stop beating. It's that simple."

"The only darkness left in my heart is hatred and a thirst for revenge against Abaddon and Alvar." She crossed her arms. "I thought that nasty drink told you that."

"The drink will only remain in your body until it passes. The implant is permanent, unless we remove it." She turned and handed Marshal what resembled a watch with a leather band. "This will enable you to communicate with us. Press the face and talk. We'll hear you."

"Do we have a plan?" Marshal asked, hooking the device to his wrist. "There must be a reason for all this."

"There is. We want Alvar and Abaddon to know that Kasdeya is now with us." She smiled. "Agatha, fetch the ball. Once he knows, then we will make sure that Kasdeya is seen openly at our side ridding the world of evil."

"She can't fight."

"Then she will learn."

"I can shoot." Kasdeya glanced at each face. "I'm very good with a gun, or at least I used to be."

"A sniper rifle might be good for her," Pierce added. "Then, she'll be able to stay back from the actual fighting like Hanna does."

"Does this suit you, Kasdeya?"

"Yes."

"Armor?" Marshal raised an eyebrow.

"I'll speak with the dragons, Marshal, but I cannot promise anything." Shayna had Agatha set the navy-blue cloth-covered ball on a small round table, then waved for Kasdeya to come close. "Remove the covering and stare into the ball. Alvar must see your face."

With a trembling hand, Kasdeya yanked off the cloth. She bent over the table and smiled. "Hello, Alvar."

A roar echoed from the ball.

Marshal pulled Kasdeya back as a bolt of lightning blasted from the crystal ball, knocking it from the table. The ball rolled across the room to the sound of Kasdeya's laughter.

"Oh, he is angry now." She clapped her hands. "Good idea, Shayna. An angry Alvar is a reckless Alvar."

4

Kasdeya

"You shouldn't be so happy about antagonizing the faerie, Alvar," Marshal said, shaking his head as he led Kasdeya to the dining hall.

She shrugged and stared at the back of Shayna's blond head and Deema's dark one. Since Deema's return to the Light, the two were inseparable. What would it feel like to have such a close friend? She glanced sideways at Marshal. Or any friend for that matter. She paused in the doorway as every faerie head turned in her direction. Other than the slight smile on Shayna's lips as she took her seat, Marshal was the only other face that passed as friendly.

"Sit here." Marshal pulled out an empty chair for her, then sat in the one next to it.

"I didn't realize gentlemen still existed."

"My mother would haunt me if I didn't pull out

a chair for a lady."

Kasdeya snorted. Lady. Ah! She hadn't been one for a long time, if ever. Still, it felt nice for someone to care enough to do such a gesture.

At the head of the table, Shayna clapped her hands to draw everyone's attention to herself. When she had it, she said, "Kasdeya has joined us in this fight. I expect all of you to extend the same welcoming courtesy to her as you did to Deema when she returned to our side. Anyone can have a change of heart as all of you are aware."

Heads reluctantly nodded. Rather than smile Kasdeya's way, they bent over their plates of food. It was a start.

Marshal patted her hand. "They'll come around."

"I doubt it," Earin muttered. "She's going to have to prove her worth."

"How?" Kasdeya sat back in her chair, food untouched. The potion she'd drunk still sat in her stomach like sludge. "How can I when minds are set against me? I understand why, and I don't fault any of you, but again, I ask how?"

The faerie shrugged. "What can you bring to the fight that will help us? Something we can't do ourselves."

Kasdeya pressed her lips together. What did she have that these people did not? What could a wealthy human do for creatures of magic? She smiled. "I do have something you don't. I can hire human mercenaries to fight alongside you. People trained to kill. I'm quite wealthy." Her words sounded like bragging to her ears.

Shayna jerked. "Bad people, and you want to bring them here?"

"People who will do whatever you tell them to for the right price." Kasdeya reached for her goblet of water. "I thought you wanted to win this war."

"I do." Shayna lifted a gold fork from next to her crystal plate. "But I'm not sure men with evil hearts are the way to do so."

"I don't think you should be picky. It sounds as if we need whatever help we can get. Besides, we can find a place in my world to train them. They won't ever need to set foot on your lands. The important thing is that they are at our side. They don't fight with the same ethics you will. They'll fight to win no matter what it takes." Kasdeya stiffened, waiting for Shayna to zap her. She should keep her mouth shut and her head down, but she couldn't defeat Abaddon on her own. She needed the faeries and their allies.

Shayna blew air sharply out her nose. "You know where to find these people?"

Kasdeya nodded. "I'll have to leave here, but yes."

"Marshal will go with you."

"You're doing this?" Earin frowned. "We don't know if we can trust this woman or the mercenaries."

"Money will buy their trust." Kasdeya returned his frown with a scowl. "As for me, only time will tell, won't it?" The man's continuous doubt sounded like a scratch on a record, repeating itself until it threatened to drive a person crazy.

"Please, we mustn't fight amongst ourselves."

Shayna motioned to the plate in front of Kasdeya. "Eat. You'll need your strength."

"You won't find any food better in this world or ours," Marshal said. "When you've finished, we'll make plans to hunt up these hired hands you're talking about."

Kasdeya took a bite of something the color of a daffodil. They were right. The food was the best thing she'd ever tasted. "What is it?"

He shrugged. "No idea. I just eat."

A laugh burst from her. Startled, she cupped a hand over her mouth. She couldn't remember the last time she'd laughed. Now that she did, she couldn't seem to stop. Tears poured down her face. Through them, the startled looks on the faces around her made her laugh harder until her breath came in gasps. When she could catch her breath, she wheezed, "Sorry."

"Are you ill?" Shayna asked, causing the laughter to start all over again.

"No, just crazy." She wiped her face with a napkin. "Perhaps I've followed the wrong side for far too long."

"Of course, you did." Shayna tilted her head. "Shall I call Nurse Ida?"

Kasdeya giggled. What was wrong with her? "No, I'll be fine. Excuse me." Still chuckling, she rushed from the dining hall, Marshal close behind her.

He gripped her arm, halting her progress. "Are you sure you're alright?"

Nodding, she smiled. "I think for the first time in many, many years, I am just fine." She hadn't cursed or wished for whiskey once since arriving in The Glen.

"I'm glad." He pulled her into his arms.

She jerked back. "What are you doing?"

"Giving you a hug. If anyone needs one, it's you."

"In my time, a man asks permission."

"We aren't in your time." He gave a cheeky grin and kept his arms out. "Come back in."

She rolled her eyes and stepped into his embrace. A hug was just what she needed, and he smelled like pine and musk, earthy, and very human.

Shayna

"Are you sure this is the smartest thing to do?" Pierce asked. "Men like she's talking about can be ruthless."

"I'd like you and Payson to be there every step of their training, as I will if I can." Shayna twirled her goblet on the table. "I trust Marshal, but Kasdeya needs watching, as will these men." In fact, she intended to be in Pierce's world overseeing things at every opportunity. "I don't want them around any of the younger girls."

"I can make sure of that," Agatha said. "I can put a charm on every female that will make them undesirable. Oh, they'll look the same, but the men will stay away and have no idea why."

"Wonderful." Shayna smiled. "Because touching will result in their immediate death. I'm serious about this."

"This means Deema and I can continue working with our warriors," Earin said. "It's a good plan."

She could only hope it worked. "We'll take the training to the human world. These strangers need to get used to fighting alongside races they didn't know existed." Ruthless people were hard to control and easily influenced. She stood and held out her hand to Pierce. "Will you walk with me?"

"Anytime, anywhere." He took her hand and let her lead him to the waterfall where she sat on a fallen log. "This place will be forever special to me." A flush rose up her neck at the memory of their binding time there. "I'm anxious for this war to be over so you and I can just be who we are meant to be."

"We are," he said, joining her. "You were meant to be queen."

"No." She shook her head. "Linette should still be here to reign. I'm only queen because of her death. I'm more comfortable with a sword in my hand."

"Hacking off the heads of demons and vampires," he chuckled.

"Yes." She joined in with his laughter, then sobered. "Am I making the right decision with Kasdeya?"

He stared across the pond. "I think so. She's still got a hard shell around her, but the Light will break through. We have to be patient and make her feel welcomed. You're doing that."

"The best I can, anyway." She stood and unhooked the clasp at her throat, letting her cloak fall to the ground. Then, she dropped her gown and headed for the water. With a coy glance over her shoulder, she invited Pierce to join her.

Binding connected them for life, much as marriage was supposed to work in the human world. Circumstances had threatened to keep her from her heart's desire, but the first thing she'd done as queen was change the law saying a queen could not bind. She'd immediately followed her heart, as had Deema. The heart didn't follow laws and should be allowed to go where it wanted.

She stepped into the cool water and continued until it reached her shoulders. Taking a deep breath, she submerged and opened her eyes. Her hair floated on the surface above her. She closed her eyes and let the cleansing water ease her worries.

Pierce's arms snaked around her middle and pulled her back to the surface. "Why are you sad?"

She hadn't realized she was until he asked. "It pains me to know more will die before this is over. Kasdeya may be saved, but the vampires will continue to convert and kill, the demons will influence madness and murder. It makes me wish tomorrow was the final battle. The one that will determine the fate of us all so it can be over."

Marshal

Upon waking the next morning, Marshal went in search of Kasdeya, unlocking the door to the room Shayna presented to her. A luxurious prison cell is how Kasdeya had described it. Marshal agreed. He saw no need for lock and key with the implant in the woman's arm.

"Ready?"

Kasdeya nodded. "May I have my gun and knife?"

"Just the knife. I'll give you the gun if you need it." He held the door open and handed her the knife. "We might as well find you a sniper rifle before approaching any mercenaries. Are you sure you have all the funds needed?"

"I'm sure." She slipped the knife into a holder on her belt. "Collecting the money is our first step. We'll need a lot of bags."

His eyes widened. "Bags?"

"You'll see." She patted his face a bit too roughly. "Come on."

Back in their world, they hailed a cab, bought several duffel bags at a sporting-goods store, and then headed into the mountains. A million questions whirled in Marshal's head, but he kept his mouth shut, letting Kasdeya remain in her thoughts. An hour later, the cab stopped on the side of a two-lane highway.

"Wait here," Kasdeya told him. "We'll be a while, but it will be worth your time. I promise."

Marshal hoped she wasn't leading him into the woods to kill him. He'd hate to be that wrong about someone he'd vouched for.

She led him to an old cemetery and into a vault

where she rolled out a cement drawer containing an elaborate coffin. Inside were stocks, bonds, cash, and jewelry. A lot of everything.

"Why isn't your money in an offshore account?"

"Oh, I have one of those, too, but Abaddon set it up, and I don't want him to be able to trace me. I may have been under his leadership, but I didn't want him to know every step I took. Once I can get it switched to a different account, I'll take the risk, then cover my tracks. Hold open one of those bags, would you?"

He slipped a duffel bag off his shoulder and held it open while she filled it, then another and another, until the coffin was empty. "We sure are weighed down."

"Yes, but we'll stash all this in The Glen under Shayna's protection and be worry free." She flashed a grin and slid the coffin back into place. "Where can I buy that gun?"

"I know an underground arms dealer who owes me a favor." Not a favor exactly, but he cooperated when Marshal needed information. It was either answer questions or go to jail. The man talked like a parrot.

They had the cab driver drop them off in front of a dry cleaners. The small Asian man behind the counter paled at the sight of Marshal. "What now?"

"I need to pick this up." Marshal slid a piece of paper across the counter depicting what he needed.

"It's this way." Yuan opened the half-door in the counter and led them into a closet, which then led them through a hidden door into another room.

"This the best." He pulled a rifle from a mount on the wall. "Marines use. Mk13 Mod 7, semi-custom, bolt-action, long-range. All you need, yes?"

"Yes." Marshal lifted the rifle. "Can you carry this?" He handed it to Kasdeya.

"With a tripod I think I can use this very well. Do you have a sling? One of those things that goes around my shoulders to hold this?"

Yuan wrinkled his nose. "Lady not know anything. I got whatever you need." He tossed a leather sling at her. "How you gonna pay?"

Marshal caught the sling in mid-air, preventing it from hitting Kasdeya. "Pay him."

The man's eyes grew the size of silver dollars at the sight of a bag full of cash. "It not safe to carry that around. Don't you watch the news? The world is ending."

"I'm here to help keep that from happening." Kasdeya smiled. "Be safe, little man." She carried the rifle out the door, leaving Marshal to jog to catch up with her.

"We need a safe place to use a computer," she said outside. "I can contact them via the internet, pay through a transference of funds online, then let them know where to come when they arrive."

"Arrive from where?"

"Everywhere."

5

Kasdeya

Working for the side of evil had its benefits. She'd acquired knowledge and resources that would now help her rid the world of Abaddon forever. She hit send on her last message and crossed her arms. "Now, we wait."

Marshal rolled a second office chair to her side. "For how long? Have you done this before?"

"No, but a long time ago, back in the early two thousands, I saw it done and memorized the code word." Stupidly simple, *For Hire*. Anyone could guess it, considering who the code was for.

Within minutes Marshal's computer set off several dings, signaling responses to her email. She flashed Marshal a grin and clicked on the first email. "Here's ten men, and…" another email showed five, and another five more. "Twenty isn't bad. I know these are hired killer—humans, but this is what they do. They fight." She sat back for a minute. "My family's old estate sits vacant. I have no idea what shape it's in, but I'll check into purchasing it, and we'll house the men there."

"Sounds like a plan."

She searched the address and gasped at the price. One and a half million dollars for something that would definitely need repair? Still, it was only money she wouldn't need when the war was over. She doubted she'd be alive to spend any. Abaddon and Alvar would put a target on her back, and every demon or vampire would be more than happy to kill her.

A phone call and wire transfer promised the house would come off the market that day. She'd have to go down and sign some papers, but that wouldn't take long. She'd have all correspondence online or through the precinct.

"You are a marvel," Marshal said, the warm look in his eyes confusing her. "This should be out of your element, considering when you were born, yet you move ahead as if you've been doing it all your life."

"It feels as if I have. Abaddon made sure I kept up with the world." Why did he look at her with admiration? Had he forgotten what she had been, what she still was? Yes, she was fighting along with those who followed the Light, but only because it benefited her. She honestly didn't know if she'd choose the same if circumstances were different.

She studied Marshal's face as he read the emails. It wouldn't do for him to fall for her. She wasn't worthy of such a man, one with a kind heart and the desire to do good because it was the right thing to do.

Nor did she belong with the people of The Glen. Kasdeya had made her lot in life, and some things could not be changed no matter how badly someone wanted them to.

"Why are you sad?" Marshal met her gaze. "You've come up with an idea that will help us all."

She shook her head. "Let's go check out the property I just bought. It isn't far from the cemetery." She marched out the door, knowing he'd follow. The man was like a dog on a leash and she held the other end. Once she'd craved power, reveled in it, but now it became a nuisance.

They made the ride to the sprawling, badly-in-need-of-fixing-up mansion without talking. They really needed to buy a vehicle. Cab fare would get expensive quickly. Now, Kasdeya stood in front of her childhood home and fought back tears.

Once stately and in good taste, one of the owners over the years had added gargoyles to the roof and painted the house shades of pink and gray. Hideous. "Let's find a way in. I won't get the keys for a few weeks."

She led Marshal to a cellar door. The rusty hinges groaned in protest as she pulled the double door open. "If we need to break in, I'd rather it be the cellar door."

The cellar door at the top of the stairs hung open, allowing them easy access to the kitchen. No appliances were hooked up, dust covered every available surface, and graffiti covered the walls. "We'll have to hire a cleaning crew and purchase appliances. We might as well see what else we need."

"I bet this place was grand once. How many bedrooms?"

"Eight bedrooms and nine baths." If they set up single beds, they'd have more than enough room for themselves and the mercenaries arriving soon. It was going to be a busy three days.

The living room and a smaller sitting room still held suitable furniture as did the large dining room. The bedrooms were another matter. Any mattress left behind had been torn apart by animals, two-legged and four. "I need your phone." She held out her hand.

Marshal handed it over and she searched for a cleaning agency that said they'd send a crew over right away. Another call hired a truck to cart away the garbage and another would send the furniture. She could see her money trickling through her fingers. Might as well keep purchasing what they needed. She ordered three armored vans with enough seating to take a crowd.

"You know, Shayna has the magic to give you an unlimited credit card."

"So there is something dishonest about her after all, as I'm sure she didn't pay any of the money back."

"How do you know that? She doesn't have a bad bone in her body. I brought it up as an alternative way to pay. You can worry about repaying if we live through the upcoming war."

"I'll do it my way." She didn't need to be beholden to Shayna any longer than necessary.

Marshal

Two hours later the house swarmed with workers. Five women carted buckets, mops, and brooms from room to room. Three burly men carted out busted-up beds and cut-up mattresses to make room for the new furniture. Marshal felt as useful as a small child.

He stepped outside and glanced at the dark clouds swirling overhead. To most eyes, it would look like a simple storm was coming, but he knew Abaddon's swarm was getting closer. They needed Agatha's protective shield before their location became known. He pressed his watch face.

"We need Agatha. Do you have our location?"

"Affirmative," Pierce said. "She'll be there soon."

Five minutes later, Deema arrived with Agatha as Kasdeya stepped onto the back patio. "I miss being able to do that."

"Step aside." Agatha brushed past her to stand in the yard. "This will take some time. This property is massive."

"What's she doing?" Kasdeya glanced at Deema.

"Putting a shield over the property to hide it. When will the workers be finished?"

"They said about three hours."

Marshal chuckled. "She can set a timer on the

shield?"

"I can do a lot of things, buddy." Agatha winked. "We'll give the mercenaries a real fright, won't we?"

His smile faded. "You can hear my conversations through the watch?"

"Of course." Deema scowled. "We need to know what Kasdeya is doing at all times. It shouldn't come as a surprise."

"Well, it does, and I don't like it." He whirled and stomped back into the house. Nothing was secret anymore. He'd have to remember to cover the watch just to go to the bathroom.

Kasdeya stepped up behind him and put a hand on his shoulder. "Why are you upset? I thought you knew how everyone felt about me."

He faced her. "Yes, but I didn't realize I'd be under a magnifying glass."

"Why not?" Her gaze hardened. "You're my guard dog. They have to make sure I don't put you to sleep." She stormed away and up the stairs.

Put him to sleep? Did she want him dead? Stupid of him to think they might have started forming some kind of a truce. Maybe he didn't want to watch over her anymore. Someone else could have the unpleasant, thankless task.

Deema laughed. "I can read your mind until the shield is up. Be careful what you wish for."

"Ugh." He moved out the front door. In order not to think any more thoughts Deema might listen in on, he called the precinct to check on matters there. "How's everything going, Charges?"

"I'm ready for the chief to take his job back,

that's how it's going. Crime is up thirty percent. Where are you guys?"

"I'm babysitting a, uh, witness. The other two are formulating a battle plan."

"Yeah, well, everyone is asking what's up. They know the world has changed and there's different types of folks around, but they still want to know what's up with you three."

"Tell them the chief is still on vacation and that Payson and I are working undercover. I'll keep you informed the best I can." He hung up to see Kasdeya watching him from the open doorway. "What?"

"I'm sorry. I shouldn't take my frustrations out on you."

"Was it hard?"

"What?"

"Apologizing?"

She smiled. "Yes, actually. It's something I need to work on. I understand I need someone keeping an eye on me. I'd do the same thing if the situation was reversed. You've got to realize the person I've been for almost a century was not a nice one. Still, if someone has to watch me, I'm glad it's you."

He stepped closer, stopping when only a couple of feet separated them. "I volunteered." He started to reach for her but backed up instead.

Deema glared at them through the window.

Shayna

Three days later, Shayna strolled through Kasdeya's home—house, mansion—she wasn't sure what someone called a building they once owned, then didn't, then did again. It would suit their purpose of housing a large number of bodies well. She intended to be here, along with Deema, Pierce, and Payson, the whole time. Agatha and the witches had insisted on coming, too, except for Rachel who wanted to stay back with her children until the time to fight came. The large house was an excellent place to train a human army. Especially with the shield.

She entered the kitchen and sniffed. Someone had brewed coffee. She really needed to have someone learn how to brew the delicious drink in The Glen.

"Here." Pierce smiled and handed her a mug. "You seem pleased."

"I am. Despite my first reservations, Kasdeya may have a good idea after all. The more fighting on our side, no matter their motive, the better." She took a deep inhale, closing her eyes.

"Things could get more complicated. Especially since we'll have some from every species training, to know how to fight next to each other. Wait until these men get a look at Gorna."

Shayna laughed. "That will be entertaining. We'll have to break them in slowly. They should arrive by nightfall, yes?"

"That's what Kasdeya said."

"Then, we'd best step outside the shield to greet

them. If they don't see a house, they might leave."

Kasdeya and Marshal already stood just inside the shield. "They're arriving in two dark vans. Once we see those, we can step out. The sky is growing darker," Kasdeya said without turning.

Shayna glanced up, spotting several demons. "We cannot. We have to send someone the demons won't recognize."

"Like who?" She asked.

"Me." Agatha joined them in the form of a Rottweiler. "If they don't faint at the sight of a talking dog, or perhaps I'll have one of them take the note from my collar."

Pierce chuckled. "That would be best."

Two vans approached.

Agatha padded forward and sat. When twenty men crowded the sidewalk, she said, "Follow me, please."

6

Kasdeya

Kasdeya laughed at the shocked expressions on the faces of twenty very large, very tough-looking men in military-type fatigues. She stepped from the shield. "Hello."

Twenty guns aimed at her chest.

Not wanting to be in the open any longer than necessary, she stepped back under the protection of the shield and waited. It wasn't until Agatha also stepped out of sight that the first two men followed, poking their wary faces through the shield. Their eyes widened, then they came the rest of the way in.

One of them, Caucasian with a shaved head, frowned, then said, "tell the others to come on through."

The other man did, and soon all twenty stood and stared at the group in front of them. The bald man, obviously the leader, narrowed his eyes. "I've seen a lot of things in my day, but a talking dog and an invisible barrier are the first. Who's in charge here?"

Kasdeya glanced at Shayna. "I hired you, but she's the queen."

"The queen of what?"

"What is your name, sir?" Shayna and Pierce stepped forward.

"William Castion. Somebody needs to start talking before we start shooting."

Agatha morphed back into her true form. "You aren't a very friendly fellow, are you?"

He paled and stumbled back, a low-muttered curse escaping his lips.

"I am Shayna, Queen of The Glen. There is a war coming that you may be able to help us win. Please, follow us to the house. You're quite safe."

Castion glanced at the men standing behind him. "You heard the lady. Let's go."

Rather than crowd the house, Kasdeya led them to the field in back where they'd be training. Paddy, the leprechaun who owned Paddy's Pub in New York, stood with Seamus, both of them wearing silly grins. Next to them Ennis, the gnome, perched on a stone bench and waved. Chairs had been placed in a semi-circle around the lawn. "Sit, and Shayna will explain."

"We'll stand." Castion still clutched his rifle. "America has no queen."

Shayna took a deep breath. "I'm a faerie, same as Deema here. You'll be fighting alongside faeries, leprechauns, witches, dragons, sprites, gnomes, and a few giants. You'll be fighting against demons and vampires. I'm sure you're aware of the so-called climate change affecting your world?"

He blinked several times. A muscle ticked in his jaw as he continued to stare.

"Go ahead and show him, Shayna." Pierce laughed. "It took me some convincing, too. I'm Chief-of-Police Pierce Cochran. These two men are Detectives Marshal and Payson. Kasdeya here, the one who hired you, is also human."

Deema grinned at Shayna. "*Shreank.*" The two shrunk in size and perched on Pierce's and Payson's shoulders.

Castion swallowed hard, lowering his gun. "You're serious."

"Deadly serious," Kasdeya said. "If this world falls under the darkness, all worlds fall. Will you still fight with us knowing whom you're fighting with?"

He faced his men. When they all gave reluctant nods, he turned back. "You're paying us, so yes. Did you say dragons?"

"We did, but this place is not large enough for them. These are the ones you'll be fighting on the ground with. More faeries will join us tomorrow." Kasdeya motioned to the house where the other witches had gathered on the porch. "Gentlemen, meet the witches. You've already met Agatha, the most powerful of them. The others will place charms of protection on you and keep you fed. Welcome to the madness."

Shayna

Shayna turned back to her normal size and watched as twenty silent men headed for the house. "I feel as if I'm always introducing myself as something out of a storybook."

Pierce put his arm around her shoulder. "You are. Let's go in. I'm sure the men will have a lot more questions once they've had a minute to absorb it all."

"You're right." She waved the others in and joined the chaos in the kitchen as the witches showed off their skills.

Spoons stirred pots of stew with twirls of fingers. Bread kneaded itself on the counter.

"We thought it best to let them see right off what we can do." Agatha waved her hand and plates flew from the cupboard and onto the dining room table. "I like it when men are speechless."

Castion sank heavily into a chair and rubbed his hands down his face. "This is a nightmare. My sins have come back to haunt me."

Agatha put a hand on his shoulder. "Buck up. You're a soldier."

He glared up at her. "You're lucky you're an old woman."

"Or what?" She wagged her eyebrows. "I'm the one who can cast spells. If you shoot me, I'll reverse the bullet back to you." She winked at Shayna.

"Enough." Shayna sat at the head of the table. "Ask your questions with an open mind. You'll hear a lot you'll be wary of."

"For one, you didn't hire us. The woman in red leather did. We answer to her."

"Shayna is the boss here," Kasdeya said. "I just provided the funds. You'll do as the faeries and detectives say."

He shrugged. "Okay. What's causing the darkness?"

Shayna folded her hands on the table and locked gazes with him. "Abaddon, leader of the dark. He controls the demons and undead."

One of the mercenaries rushed to the trashcan and vomited.

"Ignore him. He's a new recruit." Castion leaned his folded arms on the table. "How do we kill these…demons and vampires?"

"With silver. Silver kills almost everything except faeries. You'll be outfitted with the proper weapons. I apologize that we cannot give you the armor we wear." She stood, crossed her arms and jerked them down, showing him her armor.

His eyes widened. "Impressive, but we have gear to wear. It's served us well in the past." He glanced at Pierce. "You have this?"

"Something similar, but you have to have a dragon give you the scales for something like what Shayna wears."

"Huh." He shook his head. "So, we'll fight this war like any other?"

Shayna nodded.

"Then, I guess you called the right men. When do we start?"

"Once training is complete, we'll lay the trap for Abaddon. His main minions are a traitorous faerie named Alvar who has powerful magic, a vampire named Radella, and a shape-shifter named Linc. He becomes a black panther.”

“So no petting.” Agatha cackled.

He scowled. “Is she always like this?”

Shayna smiled. “Yes, isn’t she wonderful? Agatha keeps our hearts light in these dark times.” She stood. “Eat. There are rooms upstairs for you to rest. Tomorrow will be a hard day. You think you’re battle-ready, but you haven’t fought against faerie warriors.”

“Bring it on, lady. I’ve seen women run crying from a fight.”

“Oh, good.” Shayna’s smile widened. “I’ll take you on myself.” She strolled from the kitchen and onto the back porch. She looked forward to sparring with the mercenary. Leaning on the porch railing, Shayna stared at the forest behind the mansion. Kasdeya owned some beautiful property, one perfect for keeping the mercenaries out of The Glen. “He seemed quick to understand,” she said when Pierce joined her.

“I think he’s withholding judgment for now.”

“He’ll see clearly enough tomorrow. I’ll open his eyes before we spar.” They all needed to be able to see what they were up against, same as she’d done for Pierce and the other two detectives. “Nothing is simple in war.”

“No, it isn’t.” He put an arm around her waist. “You’re a great leader. We’re lucky to have you. I’m thankful I was the one to meet you in that alley.”

“You were a bit cocky and distrusting.” A smile

teased her lips.

"You didn't make much sense at first. Not until you learned the ways of my world."

She leaned her head against his shoulder. "I'm glad the Light brought me to you."

"I'm glad you changed the silly law about the queen not being able to bind with anyone." He tilted her face to his and kissed her. "I love you, my faerie queen."

Marshal

As the only single man of Shayna's group, it fell on Marshal to keep an eye on the mercenaries during the night. Ten men to a room, with him crowding in wherever there was an open bunk. Since Castion led the others, Marshal chose a bottom bunk in the same room as him.

He lay on his mattress, surprised at the comfort, and stared at the bottom of the bed above him. Kasdeya hadn't spared any expense. Good. A well-rested man was a better fighter than a tired one. He closed his eyes to the mental vision of a pretty, red-haired woman with a chip on her shoulders.

The scuff of a shoe woke him. Leaning on his elbow, he watched Castion leave the room. Marshal slipped his feet into his shoes and followed the man to the back porch.

Castion lit a cigarette. "I need a drink."

"Spend enough time with Shayna and you

won't." Marshal leaned against the railing. "I used to crave those things, but the Light takes away the urges somewhat." He still imbibed on occasion, especially when they all gathered at Paddy's.

"I have a feeling she's going to make me want to drink more." He blew a grey plume of smoke into the night air. "I've always considered myself a hard man. One with his head on straight, then I get hired to fight a war I didn't know existed with creatures I'd heard about as a kid."

"It takes getting used to."

"Tell me about the blonde."

"She's the faeries' best warrior, and now their queen. The last queen died when Alvar destroyed the palace. There was a co-queen, but she went into exile, no longer having the heart for the fight."

"The dark hair?"

"Almost as good of a fighter as Shayna. She once followed the dark but returned to our side and is now bound to Payson." Marshal cut him a glance, knowing his next question.

"The red?"

"A former demon stripped of her humanity, then cast out of Abaddon's shadow and reverted to a human again."

"Tough, huh?"

"Like a coconut."

Castion stubbed out his cigarette on the railing. "A nut you'd like to crack unless I'm mistaken."

"You aren't."

"How many on the other side?"

"Legions."

He stiffened. "How many on our side?"

"Lots."

"There's a big difference between lots and legions." He lit another cigarette.

"There is. It's likely you'll die in the battle, same as I, but the human race is at stake." That's the thought that kept Marshal going despite overwhelming odds.

"I've never much cared for humanity." He took a drag.

"I happen to care for my fellow man very much." They fell into several minutes of silence until spotting Kasdeya wandering the grounds.

"What's she up to?" Castion asked.

"Memories, maybe. She grew up here. Don't worry. She can't return to the other side without dying. Agatha gave her an implant that will kill her if she does."

The man spun to face him. "That's harsh. We should all be given the chance to make our own choice."

"Kasdeya did. She joined us, but Abaddon is powerful and may still have influence over her. You'd best be careful, too. Any darkness in your heart can be used against you." With that, Marshal stepped off the porch and followed Kasdeya.

7

Shayna

Shayna gripped her sword. She'd lost sleep thinking of how much pleasure she'd get showing Castion what a female could do on the battlefield. She changed to her armor.

"No fair." He narrowed his eyes. "I've never fought with a sword and don't have armor."

"This is for intimidation." She grinned. "My sword cannot harm a human." She held up her weapon. "You'll most likely start off shooting, but the fight will get up close. You need more than a knife for this hand-to-hand combat." She lunged.

He held up his sword as a shield. "I didn't see that coming."

"I'm fast. You're slow. Get faster." She whirled, bringing her sword around to his neck, stopping the blade a hair's breadth from his skin. "Perhaps it would be better for you to see how a warrior fights before tackling one."

"Yeah, I think it would." He stepped back.

Deema took his place. "Watch and learn."

The clash of swords filled the lawn. Soon, every man, woman, and fae gathered in a circle and watched. Shayna laughed. Oh, she'd missed doing this with Deema.

Their fight lasted well over an hour before a kick from Shayna knocked Deema's legs out from under her. She sheathed her sword. "That, Mr. Castion, is how it is done." She motioned to Logan. "Perhaps this boy will be more your speed."

Rachel's teenage son stepped in front of Castion. "I'll take it easy on you."

"Are you a faerie?"

"Nope. Just a fifteen-year-old boy who is going to kick your butt. I've been training for days."

Castion barely had time to get his sword ready before the boy made his move. Cheers and taunts from his men rose over the sound of the sword fight. Twenty minutes later, Castion caved. "Okay. I get your point. Men, pair up. We've a lot of work to do."

After Hanna showed them her skill with a bow, and Shayna and Deema showed some bolts of lightning, training got tough. Shayna and Deema moved among the trainers giving pointers, sometimes stepping in, until the sun hung high overhead.

"Take a break. Agatha. The shield for a moment, please." Shayna turned to the mercenaries. "I'm going to allow you to see some of what you'll be fighting. You need to be able to see them to destroy them. Tomorrow, I'll take you into the city to fight vampires."

"We won't be ready for that." Castion collapsed onto the grass.

"You won't be alone." Shayna stood over him. "You have to know what you're fighting."

Kasdeya plopped down beside him. "I hate sword fighting. Give me a gun."

"Same as this man, you need both." Shayna pointed overhead to a hole in the shield where five demons flew. "Agatha, take care of them."

The witch raised her palms and blasted the demons into ash before repairing the shield. "That's how it's done." She grinned at Castion.

He rolled his eyes. "I don't have any magic."

"I sense some fae in you. Hold out your hand." Shayna held her palm over his. It glowed red. "A bit of giant, which explains your stature."

"Magic?" He stared at his hand.

"No, you're just big." She patted his shoulder. "Fifteen more minutes, then back to training. The other faeries will be here soon. We'll pair each of you up with one."

The witches handed out sandwiches and thermoses of water as Shayna continued talking. "In battle, our first line of defense will be bullets, arrows, and magic. Then, we change to swords. Pierce has knives that when thrown will return back to him. Once we get to the close fighting, do not break ranks. You cannot let your group be separated. That will be certain destruction for you."

"We know what rank means," Castion said, gulping from his thermos. "Lady, I thought I knew fighting, but you've given me a new appreciation. I'll follow whatever order you give and so will my men."

"Good." She headed for the porch as Castion asked Pierce if she ever tired. Pierce said no, but Shayna did. Even then, exhaustion weighed on her limbs. She settled into a cushioned porch chair and closed her eyes. Ten minutes' rest would be all she needed.

"Sleeping on the job." Earin appeared at her elbow. "It's hard landing outside the shield without being seen."

She opened one eye. "Were you successful?"

He nodded. "We landed in the woods. Good tree coverage. How are the humans?"

"Poor with a sword. I want you pairing up with the leader. The large bald man. Don't hurt him, but don't go easy on him either."

He grinned. "You can count on it, but I'd hoped for the demon."

"She is no longer on that side."

"Old habit."

"I'll train Kasdeya. Alvar will come for her. She needs to be as good as she can be." There went any idea of a rest. Shayna pushed to her feet. "Break's over."

Kasdeya

Of course, she'd have to fight the best. Kasdeya

groaned as Shayna took up her sword and grinned.

"Why can't I go against one of the men?" Kasdeya rose to her feet.

"You need to be good. Ready?"

"As ready as I'll—"

Shayna swung her sword.

Kasdeya yelped and leaped back. "Warning, please."

"You won't have a warning on the field." She lunged.

Kasdeya parried, her palms sweating. "You make me nervous."

"I won't hurt you."

"But you want to."

Shayna lowered her sword. "No, I—"

Kasdeya whirled, bringing her sword down across the faerie's shoulders. "Never trust the enemy." She grinned.

"Touché."

They fought in earnest until Kasdeya's arms threatened to fall off. Still, she kept going. Shayna was right. She couldn't stop in the middle of a battle. "I…want…to go…with you…tomorrow." Her legs buckled, and she fell.

Shayna stopped. "Why?"

"So Alvar knows seeing me in the ball wasn't a trick." She pushed to her feet, every muscle screaming. "I've only ordered vampires, not fought them. I need first-hand experience, same as Castion and his men."

"I agree." She raised her sword. "Continue."

"Will Agatha give me a charm?"

"I'll make sure of it." Shayna sighed. "Come

with me. It's obvious you're distracted."

Kasdeya followed her into the house, to the room Shayna shared with Pierce. Hanging on the closet knob was a chain mail made of tiny links woven together.

"You were right about no dragon wanting to give you scales, so I had our forgers craft you this. Wear it under your clothes at all times, the head piece, too. No one will know you're wearing them, and they should keep you safe from being turned by a vampire. You're human now. All it takes is one bite."

She ran her hand over the smooth links. "When were you going to give it to me?"

"The first time you went out from under this shield. I guess that time is now." She left Kasdeya alone to don the armor.

The metal felt cool to her skin, but otherwise so light she couldn't tell she wore it. She glanced in the mirror. Amazing. There was no sight of the helmet or the mesh that covered her neck. Not for the first time she wished she possessed magic.

When she returned to the field, the training had stopped. Tired bodies littered the lawn. She could relate. Every step she took was agony.

"Drink this." Agatha thrust a glass into her hand.

"What is it?"

"Something to take away your aches and pains. Everyone has a glass. It isn't poison."

Sure enough, everyone who had trained that day sipped at a red plastic cup of the same vile-smelling liquid Kasdeya held. Wrinkling her nose, she emptied the glass down her throat. Relief from her aches filled her. "I hope you make gallons of this for the battle."

"We'll be prepared. Do not worry." She waved her hand over Kasdeya's head. "A charm to make you less noticeable to Abaddon and his dominions. At least you no longer glow red."

"I glowed red?"

Agatha nodded. "That's how Shayna always knew where you were."

"Thank you." Tears sprang to her eyes. "Everyone is being…kind."

"Well, that's a lie, and you know it." Agatha's smile took some of the sting from her words. "Tolerant is more like it, but in time, kindness may come." She moved back into the house.

"See?" Marshal stood next to her and bumped her with his shoulder. "I told you everyone would come around."

"They haven't yet, but we're moving in the right direction." She stared over the railing. At least fifty assorted types of living beings gathered on the lawn. For the first time since being kicked out of Abaddon's lair, she had hope he'd lose the battle.

These people fought for a common cause. His dominions fought out of fear just as she once had. Fear of losing power, fear of death. She still thought of death on a regular basis, too often, actually. She wasn't looking forward to her final destination. Unless…no, the Light could never fully accept her after all the evil she'd done.

"Cheer up, gorgeous," Marshal said. "Nothing can be bad enough to warrant the resignation on your face. We will win this war."

She forced a smile. "I'm starting to feel we might, but old thoughts and fears are hard to leave behind."

"Let me help you." He turned her to face him. "Ever since I saw you outside the window of Shayna's hotel room, something about you drew me. Made me want to help you. Kassy, I saw something in you no one else could see. I got them to agree to let you in. Now let me in, please."

"Kassy?" She raised her eyebrows.

"My pet name for you." He grinned. "So?"

"I'll try to let you help me. It's hard when I don't even know what help I need." She searched his face, unnerved at the spark of caring in his eyes. He didn't know her. Only of her. How could he care? Was she capable of the emotion of love? For over a hundred years, she'd been filled with hate, her heart hard. Could this man soften her? Did she dare hope he could?

"You'd best get some rest," he said. "It's been a long day, and Shayna wants to leave before sunrise."

She nodded, lingering a moment more before leaving him and heading for her room. Selfish, maybe, but she'd chosen the master suite. Her house, her money, but now she wondered whether she should have given it to the faerie she secretly called her queen.

After accepting her so openly after all the times Kasdeya had tried to kill her, Shayna deserved all the loyalty and respect her position warranted. If not for this group who followed the Light, Kasdeya—

Kassy—would still be wandering the streets alone and afraid.

8

Kasdeya

Those leaving the location of her house stood in a circle and held hands. With the faeries interspersed among them, they teleported as a group to a vacant parking lot in a seedy part of the city. Kasdeya and the mercenaries fell to their knees and lost the contents of their stomach.

"Don't worry," Shayna said. "You get used to the feeling of teleporting after a few times. Stay close together and keep your eyes open."

Not ever having been on this side of the battle, fear rushed through Kasdeya's limbs. She'd seen the vampires fight, knew their strength, but she also knew what the faeries were capable of. With Shayna, Deema, and Earin, the humans should be fine, right? She wiped her sweaty palms on a discarded newspaper and withdrew her sword.

A brisk wind blew a sales flier across the lot,

causing several of the mercenaries to jump. The tough men seemed more frightened than Kasdeya.

On a rush of wind, a cloud of demons converged on them from the sky, immediately surrounding the group. The detectives whipped out their bottles of holy water and destroyed the ones closest to them. After that, the battle couldn't be called anything but a melee.

Swords slashed, cries rang out, curses were shouted. As the last demon fell, the vampires emerged from every alley and doorway around the lot. A strategic mood since the living were tired after the scuffle with the demons.

"Stand fast! Push aside your weariness. You must stab them through the heart." Shayna held her weapon at the ready. "Backs together. You can do this."

"Yes, please do show us what you can do." Radella laughed from behind the ten vampires approaching them. "Looks like you have an army of fine humans, Shayna. Ones that I will love converting to one of my kind. Hello, Kasdeya. It's good to see you again. Pity you've been replaced by me." She showed her fangs. "You order me around no longer."

Castion glanced at Kasdeya. "You used to tell her what to do? I've a newfound respect for you, Red."

"It was a dark time in my life. Literally." Kasdeya refused to give into the vampire's taunting and chose to keep her mouth shut.

"Switching to the Light side stole your tongue?" Radella laughed, the sound like breaking glass.

"Kill them all, my lovelies."

The vampires sprinted the rest of the distance as Shayna's group formed a tight circle, backs together, swords raised. With her heart in her throat, Kasdeya took a deep breath. This was it. Time to fight or die. She couldn't die yet, so fight it was.

"Hold your place," Shayna hissed as Kasdeya moved forward. "We only win as a united front."

Nodding, Kasdeya stepped back.

Radella darted toward her.

Shayna stepped in front of Kasdeya. "You fight me."

"Gladly." Radella whirled, landing on Shayna's shoulders. She bent and sank her fangs into…nothing, her teeth making an audible click against the faerie's armor. "What magic is this?" She leaped to the ground and sprinted to the back of her group. "Find an opening in their armor! They're wearing neck protection. Use your weapons."

"Afraid to fight hand-to-hand?" Kasdeya grinned. "Or is that out of your abilities?" As the new commander of the undead, Radella would not fight unless she could win. With Kasdeya gone, Abaddon and Alvar wouldn't have anyone to replace the vampire and would be forced to come into the open. "We have to get rid of her," she said to Shayna.

"We can't get to her until we get through the rest." Shayna lunged forward, burying her sword into the chest of a vampire diving at her.

"Yahoo!" Castion swung his sword, removing one undead's head before plunging his sword into its chest.

His shout seemed to uplift his men as they increased the intensity of their fight. They outnumbered the vampires two to one and used it to their advantage.

Kasdeya blinked against the dark ash rising around them as their feet kicked up what was left behind of the demons and added to by the destruction of each vampire. Her throat clogged, and her eyes watered.

By the time the last vampire had been extinguished and Radella back in whatever hole she hid in, Kasdeya's breath came in gasps and wheezes. She leaned heavily on her sword and fought to catch her breath. It couldn't be. She hadn't had asthma since…well, since she'd started following Abaddon.

"Kassy?" Marshal put an arm around her. "Shayna, something's wrong."

"No…asthma." Kasdeya leaned on him.

"I'll take her to Agatha." Shayna took her hand and teleported. "Why didn't you tell us you were ill?"

"I haven't been in a hundred years." She staggered to a nearby bench to sit and wait for the witch.

Agatha came running as fast as an old woman could and put a hand on Kasdeya's back. "I cannot cure this. She needs an inhaler and medicated steam. Rachel?"

"I'm on it." Instead of joining them, the other woman darted for the house.

"Breathe out slowly for four seconds, then let the air rush back in for two and repeat the process until Rachel gets here." She glanced at Shayna. "Someone needs to go to the pharmacy."

"Call. Get it delivered." Kasdeya released her breath and counted. Without trying, her lungs sucked in air after the release. Not comfortable or a fix, but it might keep her from suffocating until help arrived. She pulled her phone from inside her jacket and handed it to Agatha.

The others arrived and gathered around her. Agatha made the call, then handed the phone back to Kasdeya. "Get back. She can't breathe if you're sucking up all the air. Shoo." She waved her hands. "Go get something to eat."

Castion grinned. "We just won a fight with vampires and demons."

"Well, good for you. I've done that many times. Go."

Despite her shortness of breath, Kasdeya gave a wheezy laugh. Oh, how she loved laughing. She'd missed it over the years.

Marshal

Marshal kept a close eye on Kasdeya as she breathed in steam from some concoction Rachel set in front of her as she rested in a kitchen chair. What must it be like not to know sickness for over a century only to succumb after one battle?

"She will be fine." Agatha patted his shoulder as she passed. "One of Castion's men is out there waiting for the pharmacy delivery. I ordered all the inhalers they had on hand. Wonderful thing, money. You can get almost anything, can't you?"

Mary Ann, the witch who had posed as the police precinct's receptionist before stepping forward to help, said, "I've suffered from this same ailment for years. We'll keep it controlled." Now that her identity was known, the woman was content to spend her time making potions and charms, leaving the fighting to the others. With Earin taking an interest in her daughter, Becky, she no longer felt even the need to keep a watchful eye on the young woman. She said her skills were more needed over a pot of something boiling.

He gave a distracted nod. "She shouldn't fight anymore. What if another attack kills her?"

"You can't keep me from the battle." Kasdeya narrowed her eyes. "The medicine will take care of it. I'll wear a mask to ward off the dust."

It probably wouldn't hurt all of them to wear something over their nose and mouth. "I can't help but worry about you. You aren't the same as you once were."

"A good thing, don't you think?" She scowled and returned to breathing in the vapor.

The man returned with a box of inhalers and dropped it on the table. "It's weird to have to explain to someone why you're standing on the side of the road in the middle of nowhere with no house to be seen. I had to tell him I lived too far down a dirt road."

"Good thinking." Castion plopped into a chair. "Today was a rush. We did great, although there was a minute there when I thought I'd wet myself like a little kid. When that Radella bared her fangs and leaped…well, not something a man sees every day."

"You'll get used to it, unfortunately," Marshal said, keeping his gaze on Kasdeya as she took a puff from one of the inhalers. Color slowly returned to her cheeks.

"Drinks on the house." Seamus appeared in the middle of the table, waving a bottle of scotch. "Just as soon as Paddy joins us, that is. This bottle is mine. Wish we could have fought alongside you, but Ireland is still struggling. Maybe we'll hire some fighters ourselves."

Paddy appeared soon after amidst hoots and hollers of joy from the mercenaries. He set a crate of bottles on the table. The evening turned into a time of celebration. They'd not lost one member, and spirits were high.

"To the queen," Castion said, lifting his glass. "It's to her training that we're all alive."

Shayna's face reddened. "You owe me nothing. I am in your debt for your help in this coming war."

"To Kasdeya, for having the money to hire these guys." Marshal toasted her with his glass.

"I haven't felt this carefree in a long time." Kassy clinked her glass to his. "I wish Abaddon had never found me."

He leaned close to her ear and whispered, "But then, I would never have met you. You'd be long dead. Have I told you that you look mighty fine for an old woman?"

She ducked her head and smiled. "At least

something positive came out of my experience."

"There's a lot more good to come, darling." He tossed back his drink. "Nothing better than Scotch from Paddy's."

"Thank ye." Paddy grinned. "Sorry I missed the fight, but I've a business to run. We leprechauns will be there at the end."

Castion spewed his drink across the table. "Leprechaun. I should have guessed when you showed up behind me with no warning. The little guy, sure, he looks like one, but…"

"Pierce is part lep," Paddy said. "That's why he's so good with knives. Can turn money to gold, too."

Castion glanced at the chief. "Really?"

"Don't get any funny ideas," Pierce said, shaking his head. "There is no pot of gold for me to tell you where it is, but here's a wee token." He turned a fork lying on the table into gold and tossed it to the man.

"Come on," Seamus said. "It's a party. What if tomorrow never comes?" He raised his hands and rained gold upon their heads.

"I think the lady in red deserves another toast for hiring us," Castion said. "I've not had this much fun in ages."

By the time the scotch was gone and most of the men retired to bed, Marshal took Kasdeya by the hand and led her to the back porch. "I'm glad you're feeling better." He helped her settle onto a lounge chair.

"Much." She crossed her ankles. "Neither Shayna nor Deema drink liquor, do they?"

He shook his head. "Neither wants their judgment impaired. Deema has a small drink once in a while, but not when there's fighting to be done. You won't see many nights like tonight, but I'm sure Shayna felt it necessary to keep the men's spirits up. There are tough times coming."

She stared out over the dark lawn. "Strange to look across this beautiful place and know that evil is lurking. Evil that I had a part in bringing it here." She scrubbed the back of her hand across her eyes. "I've been the biggest fool, Marshal. If I'd been stronger, I would've raised my child despite how she was conceived or my parents' banishment. I should have been brave and faced the trouble I'd gotten myself into."

He put his hand over hers, entwining their fingers. "All you can do now is move forward. The past cannot be changed. Go into the future without making the same mistakes."

"How did you get so wise?" She smiled.

He chuckled. "I'm not. I was so envious of Pierce and Payson for a while for having Shayna and Deema. Loneliness almost consumed me. Shayna told me to be patient, that there was someone for me out there." He raised her hand to his lips. "I think you're that someone, Kassy."

She yanked free and jumped to her feet. "Don't be an idiot." She barged into the house.

Not exactly the reaction he'd hoped for.

9

Kasdeya

How dare he say such things? How could an upstanding man like Luke Marshal have feelings for someone as dark as Kasdeya? Even after a night of restless sleep, his tenderness gnawed at her. She kicked her shoes across the room. Never would she be anyone's "someone."

She sat on the edge of the bed, covered her face with her hands, and let silent tears slip through her fingers. No matter how much she denied wanting what Marshal offered, she did want someone to love her. A warm, caring man who put her needs above his own. A man who wouldn't dump her on the side of the road because he tired of her.

No time to feel sorry for herself. Training awaited, and from the sound outside her window, some were already hard at work. Stepping to the window, she parted the curtains.

The gnome, Ennis—she thought his name was, entertained the troops by lifting heavy things and dropping them. Not funny in the least to Kasdeya since it left big holes in her lawn. She let the drapes fall back into place, yanked on her boots, stuffed an inhaler into a jacket pocket, then stomped downstairs to join the fools in the yard.

Outside, she avoided Marshal's gaze and made a beeline for Shayna. "What is he doing to my yard?"

"Showing off mostly, but he's also showing how he plans to create craters for the enemy to fall into on the battlefield."

Kasdeya frowned. "That won't work. They'll see the holes before they fall into them."

"I think he plans on smashing a few as he builds a trench around our team. It won't stop the demons, but it will make it harder for the vampires to reach us. That way, we have more time for our arrows and bullets to reach them."

"Sounds good, in theory, but I don't appreciate the damage to my lawn."

Shayna cut her a sideways glance. "Says the woman who doesn't believe she'll live past the battle. Agatha's magic will repair the lawn."

Kasdeya huffed and stormed to the kitchen and coffee. Of course the pot was empty. She measured more grounds and pushed the button. Maybe she should have thought harder about bringing all these people to her house. She craved solitude, quiet. Now noise bombarded her from every corner.

"Good morning." Marshal leaned in the doorway.

She mumbled a good morning and washed two

mugs from the crowded sink. Being human again stunk. "Coffee?"

"Yes, thank you." He stepped closer. "I didn't mean to make you mad last night."

"Not your problem." She dried the mugs and poured them full of coffee. She stared at him over the rim of her cup, stalling until she pulled her thoughts together. When she was ready, she said, "Why?"

"Why what?"

"Me."

He gave a sad smile. "We're the same, you and I. Broken, distrustful. You've had a harder time, but here you are now, fighting on the side of the Light with me." He moved closer. "Once, I held jealousy and suspicion in my heart toward Shayna and the others, but I shoved that down deep and still chose their side. I am so glad I did. You will be too." He accepted the mug she held out to him.

"I'm not sorry. At first, I was angry. I enjoyed the life I had but grew tired of not being able to leave my fancy apartment. When Abaddon told me to kill Hanna, I couldn't. Once I woke up in the subway, I realized I was happy he'd kicked me out."

"But he was one more man who had turned away from you." A shadow passed his eyes. "I won't do that."

She shrugged one shoulder and made a noise in her throat. "Easy to say. Why don't we just take this one day at a time?"

He smiled. "That's fine, but I can't promise not to tell you how I feel. I can promise to wait until you've had your coffee."

"And no more late-night confessions."

"Okay. I'll tell you in broad daylight how I feel." He laughed and carried his coffee outside.

Kasdeya couldn't stop her smile, nor did she follow him. For the moment, the kitchen sat empty except for herself. She intended to enjoy the quiet while it lasted.

"Time to train," Shayna said, sticking her head in the open doorway.

Kasdeya sighed and stood. "When are we heading into the city again?"

"Nightfall." Shayna withdrew.

In the dark? The streets would be swarming with undead. She rushed after the faerie. "We aren't ready."

"You'll have to be. Look overhead."

The sky had darkened further, making the morning seem like late afternoon. Demons gathered by the tens, whirling overhead as they searched the area for Shayna's group. It seemed Alvar had found a new place to make his hideous creations and it couldn't be too far away. "You're going to search for his factory."

"Good word for it." Shayna grinned. "Yes. He can't be far. I doubt he's still in the abandoned mine town, but there are plenty of places in the mountains for his deeds. Today's mission is to capture one of the demons and get it to talk."

Capture one? Was she crazy? "You can't be serious."

"We had one before, but Alvar released it when he helped Radella." Shayna marched toward the training fighters. "It isn't easy to catch one, but threaten it with holy water and it usually comes along. They'd rather exist than not. Same as anyone."

"I'm learning that existing and living are two different things."

Shayna laughed. "I am glad to hear that, my friend."

Friend? Warmth flooded through Kasdeya. After all she'd done, Shayna still called her friend. Tears stung her eyes despite the smile on her face.

Marshal

Kasdeya seemed to glow as she strolled at Shayna's side, and Marshal couldn't keep his eyes off her. With each passing day, the hardness of her features seemed to soften. Whether she wanted it to or not, the Light was starting to fill her heart, erasing any trace of darkness. With happiness spurring him on, he struck with his sword at Castion.

"Slow down, man. I haven't had the training you have." The other man's face reddened.

"This is how you get the training." Marshal laughed and whirled, swinging his sword and causing the man to jump backward. "I might not have your skill with a rifle, but you don't have mine with this weapon."

The man scowled. "I can learn."

Marshal lowered his sword and stepped back. "You do know the plan for today, right? To catch a demon?"

He paled. "I heard."

"The streets of New York are horrible at dark."

"Are you trying to frighten me?"

Marshal nodded. "Is it working? After yesterday's success, a man can get cocky. We can't have that impairing your judgment. I had someone at the precinct look up your records. Dishonorable discharge from the Marines for reckless behavior that endangered your men. There's also a warrant out for your arrest. Assault?"

"Arrest me or shut your mouth."

"Stop it." Pierce stepped between them. "Castion, if you survive this battle, I'll make your records disappear." He turned to Marshal. "What is wrong with you?"

He shrugged. "Just making sure these men don't get too self-confident. My life depends on them."

"As his does on yours." Pierce waved Payson over. "You two switch partners. Marshal, you train with Deema." With that order, he strode away.

"You should know by now," Payson said, "it's never a good thing to rile up the chief."

"Whatever." What was wrong with him? Maybe it rankled him more than he'd thought when Kasdeya had left so abruptly the night before. But, this morning's agreement to see each day as it came should have soothed his hurt feelings.

"Settle down, big boy." Deema grinned as he took his place opposite her. "I don't know what you see in the woman, but she'll come around."

"What makes you think anything's wrong?" He took his stance.

"It's written all over your face." She started the sparring in earnest, shouting commands and tips until it was all he could do to follow her movements. By the time Shayna called a halt for rest, he could barely hold his sword level.

"That's how the poor soldier felt," Deema said, moving back to Payson's side.

Point taken. Marshal shouldn't take his feelings out on someone else. He took a seat on the steps of the porch and hung his hands between his knees.

"That was brutal." Kasdeya sat next to him and handed him a bottle of water. "Earin hates me."

"He hates everyone that isn't a fae."

"Well, he seems to be cozying up to the witch, Becky. Lisa and Lucille stay to themselves, pretty much like Becky used to, but now she seeks Earin out at every opportunity and vice versa."

He glanced to where the white-haired faerie laughed at something the pretty dark-haired witch said. They did seem cozy. Maybe the grim faerie was lightening up. "Love does seem to be in the air." For some anyway.

She reached over and took his hand. "Don't say anything. Just sit with me."

He couldn't like anything more than the feel of her hand in his. Well, maybe her lips on his, but he could be patient when he needed to be.

"I'm scared, Luke."

"Of tonight?"

She nodded. "Fighting them is one thing, but bringing one back here…this isn't The Glen. What if we can't keep it contained? I don't think I'm strong enough to resist a constant presence."

He gave her hand a gentle squeeze. "You can. You will. I'll help you."

She leaned her head on his shoulder. "I know."

Shayna

Shayna glanced to where Marshal and Kasdeya sat and smiled. He'd found his other half, and in time, the woman would realize it. Once, she'd thought loving someone you fought alongside with was too dangerous. Now, she realized it made a person fight harder, endure longer, whatever they needed in order to keep their loved one safe. Humans were truly a resilient race. She was proud to lead them into battle.

She strolled among the weary, offering words of encouragement. They'd worked hard that day and needed rest before nightfall. While they took their leisure, she headed for the basement where Agatha worked.

"How's the cage coming?"

"The bars are silver, not iron, as requested, and hollowed out to be filled with holy water." She waved a hand at the ten-by-twelve-foot cell. "I know iron is hazardous to faeries, so let's hope this will be strong enough. I've also put a ring of holy water one foot outside the cage. This way, if it breaks free, it'll stop. Not that it can break free."

She grinned.

"You've thought of everything."

"Of course, I have. Surprises happen." She tapped a finger against her temple. "I try to think ahead." Her smile faded. "My girl, Becky, likes that Earin fella."

"The feeling seems to be reciprocated. Does it upset you?"

"I don't want anyone toying with my witches' affections. They need to think clearly."

"Don't worry about him. He's a warrior first." Shayna circled the cell, admiring the bars set two inches apart. Nothing would be able to escape. "I'd like to grab Radella again and lock her in here with one of the minions Alvar controls."

"Won't happen. Not again." Agatha hefted a large black bag on her shoulders. The bag contained a ball similar to the one they'd left for Alvar to find. She never let it leave her side for fear the traitor would see something before it was time.

Shayna took one last glimpse of the cell before following Agatha from the basement. There was nothing more they could do until the cell held a prisoner. She glanced over the crowd of fighters, knowing they had the strength it took to make sure a demon was caught. Castion and his men, despite her earlier misgivings, were just what the group had needed to become stronger. She'd never harbored more faith in her heart than she did at that moment.

Dark days still loomed ahead. A major battle hovered on the horizon. Some of those she gazed upon might die, but the side of the Light would prevail.

10

Kasdeya

The group set out after supper. The sky darkened early now, made more eerie by gathering storm clouds heavy with rain. Damp leaves from an earlier downpour muffled their footsteps as they left Kasdeya's property. Good. Silence underfoot and cover overhead gave them an advantage in their search. Maybe they'd get to their destination, wherever that might be, unnoticed.

Kasdeya would take whatever she could get. She still couldn't get over the fact Shayna wanted to catch one of those things and store it in her basement. She shook her head and stepped closer to Marshal, amazed more every day how safe she felt with him close by.

He flashed her a grin. They'd been given strict orders not to speak, but his gaze held volumes. The man was actually enjoying the hike into danger.

She'd never understand the male species if she were to live another one hundred years.

Shayna held up a fist to stop. As one body, the large group froze, allowing Agatha in her dog form to search the area.

"This way," Agatha whispered. "I recognize the traitor's scent. He's close."

Shayna nodded, and the group moved forward.

They'd only gone a few feet before the rain started. The drops burned their skin, sending smoke up from every place it hit. Flesh, dirt, leaves…cries of pain from the living filled the forest.

Agatha reverted to her human form and cast a charm that set a shimmering umbrella over them. "Alvar."

"I want to personally put my sword through him," Deema said, wiping her hand on her pants. "Acid rain."

Castion frowned. "We can't fight that kind of magic. We never know what's coming next."

"Hush, fool. I protected you from further harm, didn't I? Trust me to do so in the future." Agatha wrapped her cloak more firmly around her. "More walking and less whining."

Castion opened and closed his mouth a few times, then grinned. "You heard her, boys. Seems we've a new boss now."

Amidst grumbling about magic, witches, and evil faeries, they again followed the direction Agatha had pointed them in. Kasdeya sighed. She wouldn't add to the mutterings, but her feet quickly grew sore. Being human definitely had its downfalls, she thought, noticing how Shayna and

Deema appeared to be as strong and full of energy as when they'd started out.

"Take a break." Shayna smiled over her shoulder. "All your mental complaining is clouding my mind."

Darn her mind-reading skills and bless her at the same time. Kasdeya plopped to the ground.

While they rested, Agatha made the rounds, healing blisters and handing out another of her vile drinks to restore their strength before taking rest herself.

Kasdeya eyed the black bag the woman was never without. How much did she fit in there?

"More than we can comprehend." Shayna sat next to her. "Please don't let your discomfort cause you to regret your decision to join us."

"I won't. I wish you'd stop reading my mind." She glanced to where Luke spoke with the other detectives.

"He's a good man," Shayna said. "And stopping what I have always done is difficult."

"I didn't know men like him existed." She leaned against a tree trunk. "I'm scared of him."

Shayna tilted her head. "He would never hurt you."

"No, but if he dies on the battlefield, I'll never get over it. This entire approaching battle is because of things I've helped do." It was past time for her to admit her growing feelings for Luke. "I've been hurt so many times."

Shayna put a hand on her arm. "I know. Life is full of pain, not only in your world, but in mine. We have faith and we fight through it. Love while you can, Kasdeya. We are not guaranteed our next breath. Take comfort in the fact that Abaddon would have done all this with or without you."

"Especially in these times is our next breath a mere hope." She locked gazes with the queen. "What if I succumb under Abaddon's power?"

"You won't." She smiled and stood. "Five more minutes, my weary friend. Believe in yourself. You are worthier than you think." She left to stand next to Pierce, wrapping her arms around his waist from behind.

Maybe someday Kasdeya would believe the faerie's words. Memories of what she'd done over the last one hundred years would take a lot of getting over.

A howl ripped through the trees before a handful of unnaturally large wolves circled them. Caught unawares, the group scrambled to pull their weapons.

Kasdeya stood alone on the outskirts of the group and stared into the blue eyes of a shape-shifter. The beast snarled and charged. Using what little skill she had, she dodged to the left and rolled. Its claws swiped air.

She sprang to her feet, sword in hand, and faced her attacker. The others in her group fared a little better, outnumbering the wolves in front of them by at least two to one. She took a deep breath. She could do this.

From the corner of her eye, she caught sight of Linc slinking in the shadows. With a primal scream that surprised even her, she lopped off the head of the wolf and spun to face the panther.

"Abaddon wants you dead," Linc said. "It will be my pleasure to bring him your head."

"Try it." Marshal leaped to Kasdeya's side. "It's two to one now."

Linc snarled. "He'll be happier if I bring him two heads." The cat hunched into a pouncing position.

"Then what are you waiting for?" Kasdeya raised her sword. "Afraid?"

"Of you?" He laughed. "I'll eat everything but the head. You'll feel every bite of my teeth."

"Stop talking and—"

A blue bolt of lightning from Shayna's fingertips sent the shifter into the trees.

Kasdeya whirled, heat rising up her neck. "I could have taken him."

"Yes, but we need a path to follow. Now we have one." Shayna waved her hand. "Let's go."

"I know you could have bested the beast," Marshal told her. "But it's always best to have someone at your side."

"Of course, but she sent him away."

"She made a good point. We've been following a non-existent trail led by Agatha's nose. Shayna now has something warm to track." He gave her a quick one-armed hug. "Let's get this over with."

Marshal

When Marshal had spotted Kasdeya facing the

wolf alone, his heart threatened to stop. Then, when Linc arrived, his heart switched to overdrive. He'd fought like a fiend to get to her side. Personally, he was happy Shayna had sent the panther running. A surprise attack was never a good thing.

They stopped at the edge of a small clearing as Linc sprinted across the meadow and into what appeared to be the mouth of a cave. Marshal frowned. He wasn't aware of caves in these mountains big enough for what Alvar created. But then again, little surprised him when it came to the traitor.

"What now?" Kasdeya whispered.

"We wait for orders from Shayna." He moved to where Shayna and Pierce conversed.

"We'll leave Castion and the others behind with Kasdeya and Agatha," Shayna said. "You three and Deema will go with me to scout out the cave. If we need the others, I'll let Agatha know. If we fall, she'll take them home to safety."

"I think you should stay behind," Pierce said. "Your world can't lose another queen."

"I agree." Deema nodded. "I can lead the scouting group."

Shayna shook her head. "No, I'm going." Her tone left no room for argument.

Marshal shrugged and followed as she led them through the protection of the trees to the cave's entrance. A foul order of rotting meat greeted them, turning his stomach. Breathing through his mouth, he stepped inside.

Shayna's palms glowed white, allowing them enough light to see a few feet in front of them.

"Stay aware."

As if they needed reminding. Marshal gripped his sword and tried peering through the darkness. From deeper into the tunnel came the sound of hissing and groans. A waft of heat blasted his face. Perspiration poured down his temples, burning his eyes. Their scouting expedition didn't promise to be easy.

Keeping close to the walls, they followed the stench until a glow appeared around a corner and groans turned to shrieks. Shayna put a finger to her lips.

Pierce waved Marshal and Payson forward. He motioned his head for them to follow, then moved slowly toward the light.

Marshal swallowed against the dryness in his throat. He figured Shayna stayed behind for safety, her people needing her and all that, and Deema stayed to protect her, but he hated going in without her power backing him up.

Pierce halted them at the doorway of a large room carved into the mountain. A huge furnace filled the center where flames licked at the feet of smaller demons hanging by their hands.

The sight filled Marshal with dread. Alvar's creations were made by torturing them with fire. He clapped his hands over his ears to halt the shrill screams and staggered backward.

Face pale, Pierce motioned for them to pull back until they'd rejoined Shayna and Deema. He explained what they'd seen. "I didn't see where he keeps them after changing them, but it has to be close."

"Can we take one of the tied up ones?" She asked.

"I don't know. We didn't think that far. It's a gruesome sight."

Shayna heaved a sigh. "We can't stop after going this far. Not without what we came for."

"It won't be easy," Marshal said. "The screams and smell alone are enough to choke you."

"Be strong," Deema said, face grim. "You've faced worse."

She unwound the silver rope from around her waist. "I'll lasso one and pull it down. The rest of you cover me."

Again, Marshal found himself choking back vomit as they watched three demons writhe in agony. He knew they were dead, not alive like humans, but to see anything treated as these were was almost more than he could take. He shrank back as Shayna formed a lasso with her rope.

She swung it in a circle around her head, then let it fly. The rope tangled around the ankles of the largest demon hanging from the ceiling. With a yank, she pulled him free and dragged him through the flames. Before the creature could cry out a warning, she clapped her hand over its mouth, sealing his lips together with magic. "Make haste," she said, as the others increased the volume of their screaming.

She dragged the squirming demon from the cave and rejoined the others. "No stopping until we reach the house. Go now, and go fast. The demons of hell are virtually on our heels." She flung the demon over her shoulders and raced away, the rest of the group close behind.

Marshal gripped Kasdeya's hand when she tripped over a tree root and held on until they reached the safety of the shield over her property. The group collapsed on the ground and fought to breathe. Kasdeya puffed on her inhaler. Marshal stared at the demon who glared with black eyes.

Shayna removed the magical gag over its mouth. "Can you speak?"

"Yessss."

"Good. We've a fine room to hold you in." She gripped it by the arm and pulled it to its feet. Not yet fully transformed, it only stood as high as her shoulder. "You owe me for saving you from torture."

"I owe you nothing." Its voice sounded garbled as if it spoke through mud.

"We'll see." She dragged the cursing beast into the cellar.

"I thought I'd seen it all," Marshal said to Pierce, "but Shayna continues to amaze me."

"She is definitely full of surprises." Pierce shook his head. "I wish she'd be a bit more clear with her plans so I'd know what to expect. One minute she's as soft as silk, the other as hard as iron."

Marshal smiled at Kasdeya, happy he had a normal human woman at his side.

11
Shayna

Shayna tossed the demon into the cage and locked the door before pulling up a chair. She sat and stared as the creature fidgeted, testing the bars for strength and drawing back in pain with each touch.

"What do you want with me?" It asked, giving up on trying to escape.

"Where is Abaddon?"

The demon blinked.

"Where are the larger demons hiding?"

More blinks.

"When will the final attack come?" She narrowed her eyes. "Answering my questions will spare you further agony." She dipped her fingers into a bowl on a nearby table, then flicked a drop of holy water at the demon.

It squealed and backed away.

"Foul creature," Deema said, joining her. "It's unfortunate we have to keep such a thing."

It spit at her.

"Where is Radella?" Shayna leaned closer, fingers raised.

"Kill me and be done with it."

"You poor thing. Don't you realize you're already dead?"

"Then send me back to hell."

Shayna sighed. "It will be a painful way to go. I'll send you to hell by drowning you in holy water." She motioned to a radio on the wall. "In two seconds, I will leave you alone, lights blasting and music about the Light playing. No, I'm not above torture of my own to get what I want." Although she detested the act, it must be done. They had to know where Abaddon's new lair was located.

"I'll tell you nothing." It squatted on the cement floor and turned away.

"Very well." Shayna pressed the on button to the radio and pulled the chain to the overhead light. "I'll be back later." She turned to leave.

"You aren't posting a guard?" Deema asked.

"It cannot escape. What is your name, demon?"

"Despair," it wailed.

She raised her eyebrows. Fitting. She left, pulling the door closed behind her and Deema.

Kasdeya stood at the top of the steps, her face pale beneath her red hair. "Despair? That's one of the worst."

"You should not be this close. Come. Let me fix you coffee." Shayna put an arm around the woman and led her to the kitchen. "Coffee can fix most anything. Sit, and let me serve you."

"I should be serving you."

"Why?"

"Because, you're…well, the queen."

"But not your queen." Shayna smiled.

"I'd like to consider you my leader." Kasdeya sat. "I owe you a lot because of your kindness and acceptance. Without it, I'd still be shunned, and on the streets, most likely a vampire by now."

"We'll never know, will we?" Shayna poured them each a glass, handed one to Kasdeya, then sat across from her. "May I be honest?"

Kasdeya nodded. "Please."

"If you'd have killed Hanna, I'd have hunted you down and cut off your head. Your sparing the girl's life showed you had good in you. You only needed time for it to come forth." She sniffed the brew in her hand and closed her eyes. "I do love this human drink."

Kasdeya laughed at the queen's rapturous expression. "Not all would be as forgiving. Deema is still skeptical, and Earin almost hostile."

"You don't need to care what they think. They will fight by your side regardless of their feelings. Concentrate on how you feel about yourself." Shayna opened her eyes and leaned forward, staring into the woman's eyes. "Dig deep into your heart and pull forth the strength you know is there. I have faith in you, my friend."

"There you go with the friend again."

"Aren't we friends?" Shayna smiled.

"I'd like to think so." She reached across the table and placed her hand on Shayna's. "Thank you."

"Rest. I must speak with Despair again." Shayna took her mug with her, motioning for Castion to follow as she headed back to the basement. "As the men's leader, it is best you see what we're up against. Stubbornness at its finest."

He shook his head, stopping at the top step. "I don't want to. I have found something I'm frightened of and, well, it's embarrassing."

"You must learn to guard your heart against these creatures. Do not be afraid. I'm with you." She opened the door and waved her arm for him to go first.

Groaning, he entered the basement and halted just inside the door. Shayna gave him a gentle nudge forward. "Surely, you aren't new to negotiation tactics?"

"No, but those are on people!" His eyes widened. "Not…things."

Shayna chuckled. "Sit, Mr. Castion, and observe, nothing more."

The demon snarled, his fangs showing white against its black skin. "Yes, human, listen to my words. You will die in this battle if you continue following this faerie."

"Silence." Shayna dipped her fingers in the bowl. "Let's go through the routine again. Where is Abaddon?"

"Turn off the music, and I'll tell you."

"Tell me, then I'll turn it off." Shayna held up her hands. "Where is Radella?"

"I don't know where either of them are." He cringed away from her. "Alvar is our leader."

"Where is Alvar?"

"Plotting to kill you."

"Where?" She drew out the word. "I want his location."

"Look into your stupid ball and ask him yourself."

Interesting. "You know of the crystal ball?"

"We all do. He showed it to usss." His gaze moved back to Castion. "Would you like to know how you die? The exact moment you draw your last breath?"

Shayna shook her head. "Don't listen to him. Guard your ears. He speaks lies."

"Do I, soldier? Look deep into your soul and tell me if I lie."

Castion cursed and rushed from the room.

Shayna sighed. Those who harbored darkness in their hearts could be so weak. Realizing the demon would tell her nothing useful, she turned up the volume on the radio and left the basement.

Kasdeya

"What happened?" Kasdeya trotted after the fleeing Castion.

"It got inside my head." He leaned a hand against the porch railing. "His words seeped into my soul, threatening to steal what humanity I have left." He lifted a tortured gaze. "No wonder you gave in so long ago."

"Abaddon was relentless in his pursuit of me. You can fight this, because you know what it is you fight against. I was young and lost."

"I'm a mercenary. I kill people for money. That's worse in my book than giving the orders for someone else to do the dirty work." He shoved away from the porch and strode out of sight.

Marshal joined her. "He'll be alright."

"I'm not worried about him." Kasdeya sat on a porch chair. "Shayna will care for him. I'd forgotten how hard being human could be."

"Don't forget how wonderful it can be, too." He knelt in front of her and took her hands in his. "We're free to love who we want, go where we want, be whatever we want. There's a marvelous freedom to being human."

He was right. Kasdeya was no longer locked into a penthouse apartment forced to do the bidding of evil. She could walk away this minute if she wanted to. She cupped Marshal's face and touched her nose to his. "You always know what to say. Careful, or you'll be as wise as Shayna."

"No one is as wise as Shayna, unless it's Agatha," he chuckled. "Are you hungry? There's something that smells wonderful cooking in the kitchen."

"I am hungry. It's been a long, tiring day."

He pulled her to her feet and led her into the kitchen where the others had already gathered, spilling over into the dining room. "Let me fix you a plate." He pulled out a chair at one end of the dining table.

While she waited, she studied the faces of the men around her. Fear and nervousness coated their features. They needed a day away from the horror of evil. She sat back in her chair and crossed her arms. One problem was solved with money, how could she solve this one? She knew, and it wouldn't cost a penny.

She pushed to her feet and went in search of Shayna. Finding her in the living room, feet on the coffee table and a plate balanced on her lap, Kasdeya stepped in front of her. "I have a request to make, and I'd like for you to hear me out before you answer."

"All right." Shayna set her plate on the table. "You have my full attention."

"The men are frightened. I don't think we should raise their spirits with liquor again, so I suggest that you, as queen, take them to spend a day in The Glen. Let them see the dragons, meet a giant, and see the other creatures they'll fight alongside. They look as if they're giving up rather than growing stronger."

Shayna pressed her lips together, then glanced at Deema. "What do you think?"

"It's a risk, but it won't be the first time we close the portal and open another one somewhere new."

"It isn't the first time humans have entered your world, and there is nowhere they spend a time regaining their faith in this one. Not without discovery." Kasdeya would press the issue until Shayna agreed. "I think they've proven they can be trusted. Agatha put a charm on the young women.

It'll be perfectly safe."

"I'd have to implement some rules," Shayna said, reaching for her plate. "I see your reasoning. Let me discuss this with Mr. Castion. Please send him to me. I will make my decision after speaking with him."

Anticipation bubbling up inside her, Kasdeya fetched Castion from the kitchen. "Shayna wants to talk to you."

"If it's about this morning, I don't want to," The man pouted.

"It isn't. Come on."

He followed her to where Shayna waited. "Yeah?"

"Please, sit." She pointed to a chair across from her. "Kasdeya presented an interesting proposition to me. It's clear that we all need a rest and a break from this place. Something we cannot do outside this shield."

"Yeah?" His brow furrowed.

She smiled. "How would you like to visit my world, Mr. Castion? Perhaps take a ride on a dragon?"

His mouth dropped open. "Are you serious?"

"Very. But there are rules that would need to be followed to the letter, sir. Plus, my people need to see me. It's been too long since I've been back."

"My men will be over the moon. I'll make sure they follow your rules."

"Wonderful. Have them gather in the yard after they eat."

Castion grinned and turned to Kasdeya. "Your idea?"

She nodded. "I know how you're feeling. At least you'll be going as an invited guest and not as someone suspicious." Still, her heart leaped to be returning to the one place she knew was the safest in any world.

"You're a good woman, Red." He rubbed his hands together and rejoined his men.

Half an hour later, they gathered in the yard. Shayna stood on the porch in order to allow them to see her. Once all eyes were on her, she spoke. "Our friend Kasdeya approached me with a request to take the lot of you on a day away from here." She smiled at Kasdeya. "After serious consideration, I've decided to do just that. In the morning, there will be several faeries joining us so we can take you to spend a day in our world. There will be feasting, dragon rides, magic, and much more." She raised her hands high against shouts of joy.

Marshal clasped Kasdeya's hand. "A good idea, darling."

She smiled, warmed by not only his words, but his touch.

"There will be rules, though," Shayna continued. "You are not to touch a single one of my faerie women, nor any other woman. You will behave as the honored guests you are." Her features hardened. "If you assault a single person in my world, you will be put to death." She clapped her hands. "Get a good night's rest and gather here after breakfast."

Kasdeya's shouts rose with the others as spirits ran high. The weary faces of those around her brightened in anticipation. Now, all she could do was hope that the suggestion she'd proposed didn't backfire on her.

12

Kasdeya

The excitement on the men's faces as they teleported to outside the portal barely diminished as they vomited into the bushes. Kasdeya knew the beauty and peace that resided in The Glen but still couldn't hold back her enthusiasm. She'd ignore any distrustful glances from those who resided on the other side of the portal and enjoy the day.

"Will we really ride a dragon?" One of the men asked.

"If they allow it." Shayna turned to face them. "I must enter first to let the others know you are coming. Deema will come last to guard the rear. One-by-one you will step through and stand by my side. I will give you further instructions then. Kasdeya, you come after me." Shayna ducked under a low-hanging branch of an oak tree and stepped through its trunk.

Taking a deep breath, Kasdeya followed, stepping onto a lawn so green it hurt her eyes. A group of faeries, their arms loaded with baskets of fruit, stood as a welcome committee. They bowed at Shayna's feet, casting Kasdeya only a cursory glance. It seemed as if they'd had prior warning of her visit. How wonderful, though. They no longer shot daggers in her direction every time they looked at her.

As the others joined them, Shayna explained to her people the need for a group of large human men to enter their land. The faeries nodded in acceptance and strolled among the visitors holding out their baskets.

The men accepted the offering, none of their gazes lingering on the beauty of the female faeries. Kasdeya smiled. Agatha's charm of making the females undesirable worked.

"How did Pierce and Marshal get the only good-looking women here?" Castion whispered, glancing at the apple in his hand. "Is everything this colorful?"

Kasdeya laughed. "You won't taste better." She stepped away and stood at Marshal's side.

"She's summoned Gorna," he said. "The dragon will let us know if any of the others are willing to give something akin to a pony ride."

"It'll be anything but a pony ride." Kasdeya held no hope she'd receive a ride. Dragons, she'd heard, could carry grudges longer than anyone. Not that she'd personally attacked one, but they would know of her, and that would be enough to deny her in their eyes.

"Relax," Marshal said. "Enjoy the day of rest. If nothing else, it's great food, beautiful surroundings, and a day off from the dangers we face."

"You're right. I intend to make the best of things." She slipped her hand in his, immediately feeling the tension disappear.

Shayna led the group on a tour of the land, the waterfall, pointing out the mountains rising in the distance. "We are hidden from evil here, now that Alvar has been banished. Look." She pointed to what at first appeared to be a bird but soon turned into a dragon with scales so bright and blue they almost blinded the humans. "Meet Gorna, whose scales made my armor."

The dragon landed with a thud, vibrating the ground under their feet. Her large head turned to Kasdeya. Her eyes narrowed.

"She's one of us now, my lovely friend." Shayna patted the dragon's neck. "Will you let her ride with us? Will you call the others to give our other friends a day they will never forget?"

Gorna hesitated, then nodded and lay flat to allow Shayna and Kasdeya to climb on her back.

"Really?" Kasdeya's breath caught. "I can ride her?"

Shayna held down a hand. "Yes. Let's show the others how it is done."

Kasdeya gripped her hand and let the other woman pull her up. Wrapping her arms tight around Shayna's waist, she'd never noticed before how she smelled of flowers. She grinned down at Marshal. He gave her a thumbs up and stepped back as Gorna flapped her wings.

Kasdeya shrieked as they took flight, relaxing as they soared through a sky so clear, air so pure, it brought tears to her eyes. She'd never enjoyed anything more than the time they flew over The Glen. Those below waved as they dipped over their heads. Tears spilled down Kasdeya's cheeks. This was the final acceptance. Gorna's agreement to let her ride would prove to all the others she was truly a woman of the Light.

"Thank you, Shayna. More than I can say."

"You are most welcome." Shayna leaned close to Gorna's ear. "Hang on!"

The dragon rose higher until nothing was visible below them but clouds. Gorna flew up and down as a dolphin leaped through the waves of the sea. Happiness welled so strong, so full, Kasdeya thought her heart would burst.

When they landed, she knelt before the dragon and reached up her hands. "Thank you." The words seemed so inadequate for what had transpired. When she stood, the faeries no longer glared, no longer sent her impassive glances but smiled and clapped.

Shayna slid from Gorna's back and put her hands on Kasdeya's shoulders. "Rise, my friend. You are one of us."

She stood. "Your dragon is as kind and noble as you."

Gorna's golden eyes sparkled.

"She agrees," Shayna said, laughing. "Here come your rides, gentlemen." She waved an arm at the sky filled with dragons in every hue of the rainbow. "Enjoy. Afterwards, we eat."

Cheers rose as the dragons landed and men clambered to claim their ride.

Shayna

As the others sat around tables set up outside, full of food and drink, Shayna listened to their amazement at having ridden a dragon. She'd grown up seeing the wonders of her world and loved seeing them for the first time again through the eyes of another.

Seamus had brought several of the leprechauns to dance a jig upon the tables as the others ate. Ennis, the gnome, entertained by lifting objects of great weight into the air and lowering them slowly so as not to damage the ground. Sprites, their tiny voices raised in song, flitted among those at the tables and sang a lilting melody.

Today seemed more of a celebration than a day of rest. The type of day one might have after winning a battle. She wrapped her fingers around a crystal goblet, sorrow flicking through her heart. Some of those in front of her might not live to see another celebration.

"Why so sad?" Deema asked. "It's a wonderful day."

"Thinking of the war."

"Don't." Deema smiled. "Think only on today. The war will still plague us tomorrow." She turned as the ground trembled under their feet.

Three giants marched their way, towering high over them all. The largest of the three, a woman, bent one knee to come closer to making eye contact with Shayna. "I am Olga. We come to lend our aid."

Shayna stood. "And you are welcome."

"That is some kind of woman." Castion raised a glass.

Olga turned and, using her thumb and forefinger, lifted him by the neck of his shirt. "Show respect to one who can squash you like a gnat, little man."

"He's part giant," Shayna explained. "Hence his forthright speech."

The giant's laugh boomed, and she set Castion on her shoulder. "A kinsman. It is good to meet you."

His wide eyes stared down at Shayna. He mouthed, "help."

She laughed. "You've made a friend. Olga, this is Castion, the leader of these fighting men. Are you hungry?"

"We are always hungry."

"Agatha?" Shayne turned to the old woman.

"Under control." She cast a spell that caused the food to grow to enormous amounts, sagging the tables under the weight.

Olga set Castion down and sat cross-legged on the ground, upending platter upon platter into her mouth. Shayna hoped the rest of the group had finished eating since there'd be nothing left.

"Will there be more of you coming," she asked the giant.

"No idea. We do as we will." She belched, ruffling the hair on those across from her. "I do enjoy faerie food even more than ours."

Shayna laughed. "Of course, it's better. You eat sheep alive."

"True." She pushed to her feet. "Enjoy the rest of the party. We sleep after we eat and there is no room for us to stretch out here. We will stay with the dragons." As abrupt as they'd arrived, the three giants left.

"That's good for us, right?" Castion asked. "The giants fighting?"

"Very good." Shayna clapped her hands and the day turned to night.

The sprites now glowed like blue lightning bugs. The leprechauns' dancing turned to music instead as they pulled musical instruments from bags they'd brought. Each of the faeries grabbed the hands of someone else and dancing commenced.

By the time night had fallen in the human world, the partiers were tired, happy, and ready to face whatever the next day might bring. It was a happy group Shayna returned to Kasdeya's home. Yet, rather than retire to their beds, they found a patch of grass to sit on and reminisced about the day.

"I see more clearly what you're fighting for," Castion told her. "Your world is wonderful. Someday, I hope mine will be the same."

"It will. For a while after the final battle is won." But then, the evil in men's hearts would grow again, and Shayna's people would again come to their aid.

"If we win."

She sighed. "I tell the others we will, but you are a military man. You know what I hope and what will happen can be different. Darkness grows daily, but until we have Abaddon chained, we cannot hope to beat Alvar and his minions."

"Maybe it's time to speak with Despair again. When we torture, we waterboard and pull out fingernails."

A laugh escaped her despite the gravity of the situation. "The only water that will hurt Despair is holy water. If we waterboard, it will die before giving us any answers. I for one do not want to get close enough to pull out its claws."

He shuddered. "Neither do I. My next question is…what next?"

Shayna glanced around her group of fighters. "We keep searching for Abaddon."

"I have an idea where he might be. At least, where I might hide if I were as evil as he is."

She leaned to peer into his face. "Where might that be?"

"Pilgrim Psychiatric Hospital on Long Island. Abaddon strikes me as an egotist. Where better to hole up than the worst place ever created on earth?"

Shayna's blood ran cold. He could be right. An abandoned, presumed haunted place, famous for atrocities against humankind would be an ideal place for one such as Abaddon to hide. "What brought this place to mind?"

He plucked at the grass under him. "I've relatives sent there who died. It's the worst place I can imagine being, other than hell."

"Come with me." She sprang to her feet and

headed for the basement. She'd have her answers that night, one way or the other.

"Despair!"

"I'm here."

Shayna stepped up to the bars of the cage. "So, Abaddon has turned Pilgrim."

The widening of the demon's eyes was all the answer she needed.

13

Kasdeya

"Are you sure?" Kasdeya's hand paused in lifting her coffee mug to her lips. "I've seen the things that place does firsthand."

"I am sure. We will not leave without Abaddon in chains." She turned to Agatha. "You have the chain in your bag?"

"I do. It's heavy." Agatha hefted the bag. "It will have to be a small group, Shayna. We'll never get close enough if we bring everyone."

"It's you, me, and Kasdeya."

"What?" Kasdeya's hand shook hard enough to spill coffee down her black shirt. "Why me? I'm the weakest one here."

"Because you know him the best. Once we get there, you'll be the best judge of where he might be. The place is large."

No, no, no. She couldn't face him again. Not

without a large group of warriors between them. "I can't."

Shayna narrowed her eyes. "You can, and you will." With that, she marched from the kitchen.

"She's already had this argument with Pierce who didn't want to stay behind," Agatha said. "The three of us can handle Abaddon. He cannot escape these chains once bound. Stay with us, and you'll be fine."

Kasdeya felt again as if she had to remain at Shayna's side in order to be watched. What possible use could she be to the other two? She checked her pockets for her inhaler, stalling before she joined the others outside.

Marshal put his hands on her shoulders from behind. "Promise you'll return to me."

"I can't make that easily with only the three of us going." She turned and wrapped him in a hug. "I don't want to go, Luke."

"You're going with two of the best." He rested his chin on the top of her head. "I'll see you later." He tilted her face to his. "Shayna wouldn't be taking you if she didn't need to."

She hoped he was right. On her tiptoes, she placed a kiss at the corner of his lips. "I'll give you a real kiss when I return."

His lips curled into a smile. "I'll be looking forward to it." Taking her by the hand, he led her to the back porch where the others waited.

Shayna glanced up from her goodbyes with Pierce, then cupped her man's face. "I'll see you later."

He nodded, swallowing hard. "Until later. I love

you, my faerie queen."

After kissing him, she turned a grave look on Kasdeya. "We'll be teleporting. I trust you're wearing your chain mail?"

"I am." She squeezed Luke's hand.

"Wear this. Never take it off." She handed Kasdeya a silver cross necklace. "It will help." Shayna held out her hands to Kasdeya and Agatha. The moment they touched, she teleported them outside a massive brick building. Four stories high and spreading across a lawn filled with weeds, the sight struck fear in her heart.

Kasdeya slipped the necklace over her head and tucked it inside her shirt.

"Stay close and stay low." Shayna led them to a side door, then stepped aside for Agatha.

The witch spread some type of greasy substance on the hinges and the door swung open without a sound. They stepped into a common room filled with worn, overturned furniture as if a riot had broken out seconds before the building was condemned.

Kasdeya shuddered, feeling the spirits of hundreds of lost souls trapped within the walls. A blue sofa, its stuffing hanging from multiple holes, no longer beckoned for someone to sit and stay awhile.

Long ago, she'd sat on that very sofa, posing as a nurse. Abaddon had wanted Radella, one of the patients. After discovering Radella had been captured and committed because of her fangs, it hadn't taken long for her to start turning patients and staff into vampires. Kasdeya had confronted her and told her of Abaddon's need. It was the only thing to keep her from turning Kasdeya into one of them.

Now, here she was again on another search for one of evil's most devious. They headed down a hall of chipped plaster walls and rutted marble floors, past once-curtained doorways that held those chained to their beds. This place hadn't had a chance against Radella.

Shayna stopped at the foot of a set of stairs. "Where do you think he'll be?"

"The tower. Abaddon will want to be where the most atrocities took place."

"There is still evil here," Agatha said. "It makes my skin crawl."

"You should have witnessed it firsthand." Kasdeya put a hand on one of the railings and found herself propelled backward into a wall. The breath left her lungs in a whoosh.

"Don't touch anything," Agatha hissed. "Alvar will have set traps."

Now she told her. Kasdeya crept to her feet and dug her inhaler from her pocket. A puff later, she followed the other two up the stairs. She'd forgotten how big the asylum was, halls veering off in all directions.

She glanced through an open doorway to where an empty, rusted tub sat. Tears sprang to her eyes remembering the old woman who'd been held under the water a bit too long. Not by her hands, but she'd been a witness and stood by and done nothing.

The sound of a scuff overhead drew their attention, and Shayna held up a hand for them to halt. When no other sound came, they continued.

Kasdeya barely had time to face the vampire as it attacked. She brought up her sword on instinct, plunging the blade into the creature's chest before a sound escaped either of them.

Shayna gave a nod of approval and turned down a hallway to their right. Their feet splashed through puddles of water from the prior evening's rain.

They stopped at another set of stairs, and Shayna faced Kasdeya.

Kadeya nodded. "If he's here, it will be up these stairs."

"It could be a trap," Agatha said.

"It most likely is." Shayna squared her shoulders. "Give me the chains."

Shayna

Shayna looped the heavy chains over her shoulder, thankful for Agatha's magic that kept the links from clanking and alerting Abaddon to their presence. Quashing down the fear rising in her throat, she climbed the stairs to meet the one once caught by Linette. The one ultimately responsible for the death of The Glen's past queen.

Only one door stood at the top and it was closed. Shayna pressed her ear against the wood and listened. The squeak of leather, the rustle of paper, both signaled someone resided on the other side. Taking a deep breath, she reached for the door handle.

The door swung open and two vampires rushed them. Shayna lost her footing, the weight of the chains dragging her down. By the time she stopped rolling, she'd landed half way down the flight of stairs they'd just climbed, and Kasdeya and Agatha fought for their lives.

Dragging the chains with her, Shayna took the stairs two at a time and stepped between the attackers and the fighters. "Come out and face me, Abaddon. Stop sending your minions to do your dirty work."

"He isn't here," one of the vampires said. "He is where you can't go." He bared his fangs and hissed.

"Then you are no longer needed." She disposed of him, while Agatha tossed a dagger into the heart of the other. "Where will we find iron?" She asked, turning to Kasdeya.

"There are cells where the most violent were kept." She tilted her head.

"We'll have to lure him out. Iron binds me."

"Then we will stay between you and the cage," Agatha said. "Come on. Time is wasting, and I don't put it past the man to flee."

"How far, Kasdeya?" Shayna headed down the stairs at a run.

"The other side of the compound."

Wonderful. They'd meet more of the undead between here and there. "Agatha, the strengthening potion, please."

"We don't know how it will affect someone who once followed the dark."

"We don't have a choice. She cannot arrive to

capture Abaddon when weary." Shayna stopped at the bottom. "Will you risk it?" She faced Kasdeya.

"Be stronger or die? Sure, what kind of choice is that?" She gave a wry grin.

"Just a sip." Agatha glared up at Shayna while handing the vial to Kasdeya. "If you live, I'll give you another in a few minutes."

Shayna watched for signs the potion would not work as Kasdeya took a sip. When the woman seemed to suffer no ill effects, she ordered her to take another sip. "I'm sorry for risking you this way, but the path ahead will be dangerous."

"I feel great." Kasdeya took a larger sip.

"Good." Shayna smiled and set off at a faster pace toward the tower on the other side of the grounds.

They met three undead in the common room where they'd first entered the building. They weren't well-trained or disciplined, which led Shayna to believe the better-trained vampires were being held for the final battle. These were nothing more than a distraction to slow her down.

The second tower rose identical to the first, and they barged up the stairs no longer concerned about stealth. Abaddon had to know they were there. They burst into a room in which sat a large iron cage. Inside the cage sat a handsome, silver-haired devil by the name of Abaddon.

He stood and smiled. "We meet at last, my lovely new queen, and you've brought friends."

Agatha waved a hand and closed the door, sliding the latch. "No need for more in our little party."

"I'd like to have a witch in my army. Why don't you join me and enjoy all the riches that the faeries can't give you."

Agatha cackled. "I have a friend who can turn things to gold. I'm good."

His smile didn't dim, but his eyes hardened. "So, what now? Kasdeya harbors a grudge she can have no satisfaction of acting on. We have a faerie queen who cannot approach iron, and a witch happy to live in rags among the losing team."

"Hey, these cloaks are as old as you. Show some respect." While Agatha spoke, she'd circled the cage, sprinkling a powder along the bottom of each bar.

Sneaky woman. Shayna grinned. Soon, even a child could knock the bars down and Abaddon would be dragged out to become her prisoner.

Kasdeya seemed frozen where she stood, snapping out of her trance when Agatha punched her in the arm. "When I say go, knock down the bars. Shayna, drink this. You'll only have a few minutes to act."

"What's this?" Abaddon narrowed his eyes.

"Your demise," Shayna said. "I hold chains you cannot escape."

"My capture will not end this. Alvar and Radella are strong enough to cause your side to fall. When it does, they'll release me." He sat in a chair inside the cage. "Do what you will. I'm a patient man."

When Agatha gave the signal, the three women rushed the cage, knocking the bars loose. Shayna coiled the chains around Abaddon and dragged him from the room as her legs started to grow heavy from the iron. Outside, she leaned against the wall and waited for her strength to return.

Abaddon sat compliantly waiting, seeming to believe it only a matter of time before his rescue. Perhaps he was right, but Shayna would make sure those who followed the Light took down as many of his minions as possible.

Without speaking, each of the women grabbed a piece of the chain and led a silent Abaddon into the afternoon light. Rather than take him to Kasdeya's, Shayna teleported them to The Glen where she would set seven faeries to guard him. It would not be easy for him to escape this time.

Once there, she handed the end of the chain to Earin. "Take him to the dragons. They cannot fall even if we lose the war. Abaddon will never roam this world again."

"No!" Abaddon fought his chain. "Keep me here in The Glen. You cannot take me to the dragons."

"Why not?" Shayna cocked her head. The man seemed distraught for the first time since they'd found him. Had Queen Linette been mistaken and there was a way to destroy him? "You are afraid. Why?"

Kasdeya smiled for the first time since they'd left the others. "I think the only ones who can rid the world of him are the dragons. How about we go find Alvar and Radella now and leave this....thing to his ultimate demise?"

14

Kasdeya

"*You caught Abaddon?*" Marshal collapsed on the sofa. "Just the three of you?"

Kasdeya nodded. "Agatha did her magic, and Shayna twirled that length of chain like it didn't weigh anything." She sat next to him. "Then, she sent him straight to the dragons."

"What are they going to do?"

"Eat him, I hope." She grinned. "Now, to face Alvar and Radella and put this whole ugly mess behind us."

"I agree." Shayna and Pierce entered the room and sat on a love seat next to the sofa. "I'm embarrassed to say I have no idea how to lure them out."

Pierce scratched his head. "Other than inviting them to a fight, I'm clueless, too."

"So," Marshal leaned his elbows on his knees,

"we pound the pavements every night? That will be dangerous and tiring. Exactly something they would want us to do."

"A trap?" Kasdeya's blood chilled. "I'm the bait."

"No." Marshal shook his head.

"Hear me out." Knowing it would be Shayna who made the decision to act or not on Kasdeya's idea, she trained her attention on the queen. "They won't buy the fact that I would again change my mind, but what if they thought you kicked me out? Radella would come for me. Nothing would please her more than to turn me and force me to do her bidding."

"They wouldn't fall for that ploy, but…" Shayna crossed her arms, "you are known to be headstrong, so perhaps they would believe you if you set out on your own for revenge. Left the safety of this place to find them on your own."

"That might work." Pierce nodded. "It would still be dangerous."

"I don't like it." Marshal scowled.

"She wouldn't be alone," Shayna said. "We'd be following from the shadows."

"The moment Radella made a move toward me, the plan would be ruined," Kasdeya said. "I have to go alone. We'll only get one chance at this."

Shayna stood. "Then the plan would be ruined. We won't let Radella take you. Instead, we'll use you as bait to take or kill her. That would leave Alvar on his own. The vampires would not blindly follow him without their leader."

"What about the big guy, Luke?" Pierce glanced

at each of their faces. "We've not heard a thing about him since finding Alvar in that mining town. Wouldn't he take Radella's place again? We can't forget Linc either. Alvar has more than one formidable creature at his side."

"Then we pick them off one by one until we get to him." Kasdeya had thought capturing Abaddon would still the thirst for revenge threatening to consume her, but that thirst couldn't be quenched until every last one of the dark leaders had been stopped.

Shayna's eyes narrowed. "I hope this drive for revenge doesn't result in your demise, Kasdeya."

"Stop reading my mind."

Pierce laughed. "I gave up telling her that."

"It's unnerving having to guard my thoughts all the time." Kasdeya propped her feet on the coffee table.

"Sometimes your thoughts are so strong, so angry, that I can't stop hearing them." Shayna sighed. "We've agreed to try luring Alvar's followers into our trap. Marshal will go with you. If they've been studying us at all, even during a battle, they will know he cares for you. For you to venture out without him will seem strange."

"But the rest of you will still be hiding in the shadows."

Shayna nodded. "We will take the risk of the plan failing in order to keep you safe. I'm hoping if we're discovered, they will think we followed you." She grinned. "I'll have to chastise you. Pretend to be sufficiently corrected when that time comes."

Kasdeya smiled despite her annoyance at having

her mind read. "I will behave like a child receiving a lecture."

"This is not a laughing matter." Marshal lunged to his feet. "She might die out there."

"She might die on the battlefield or crossing the road," Shayna said. "Settle yourself. We all know the dangers of ridding the world of darkness. Take your rest. You will train hard tomorrow before you leave."

"Sometimes, she scares me," Pierce said after Shayna left. "I've gotten used to the mind reading and learned to control my thoughts to an extent, but when she's got her teeth in something, she's like a junkyard dog who won't let go of a bone. Kind of like you, Kasdeya."

She jerked. "I'm nothing like Shayna."

"Yes, you are." He leaned against the seat back. "You take hold of something and hold on tight."

"So?" She frowned.

"I'm just saying you're as stubborn as she is at times."

"Except Shayna's drive is for the common good while mine is for my own revenge."

Marshal put his hand on hers. "Even now? Even after spending time with these people?"

Her shoulders slumped. "No, not anymore. I've thought only of myself for so long, it's hard to believe I'm no longer that person." She glanced into his handsome face. "But I do really want revenge for the things I've lost."

He gripped her hand. "Then, you can focus on what you've gained." He stood, pulling her to her feet. "Good night, darling." He placed a kiss on her forehead.

"Good night. You too, Pierce." With a glance at the chief of police, she headed upstairs to her room.

After removing her clothes, she slid under the blankets, pulling them to her chin. She must be insane, offering herself as bait. She should have known Shayna would send Marshal with her. Now, her plan to rid the world of Alvar might result in the loss of the first man to truly love her despite who she was. A man she'd promised to kiss and forgotten.

Marshal

"She'll need to be watched," Pierce said. "I'm afraid her determination to get rid of Alvar might cause her to do something reckless."

"I'll keep her in line."

Pierce chuckled. "Said like a man who has never loved a woman before. Kasdeya is not a submissive woman. She won't take to being bossed."

"No, but maybe she'll let me partner with her in her decisions." Marshal resumed his seat. "Charges is growing tired of running the precinct in your absence. He's a uniformed officer, not a leader."

"I know. Shayna and I have discussed this. I'll have to return after my long vacation. You and Payson will have to come with me."

"It'll be dangerous."

He nodded. "But Shayna and Deema will also be with us. It will make our presence in the city more believable when Kasdeya is seen. It won't be a secret for long that you care for her, and vice versa. You'll become a target."

"No more than the rest of you. When are we headed back?"

"The three of us go in the morning. Shayna and the women will join us after training. Then, you and Kasdeya will leave the precinct and head into the streets. Earin will come here to train Castion's men."

Marshal nodded, grim determination setting his jaw. It seemed as if everyone had been busy making plans but him. He'd had his heart and mind so wrapped up in his feelings for Kassy, he'd missed all the meetings that must have been happening right under his nose.

He headed to the room he shared with the mercenaries. Morning would come too soon.

Gritty-eyed from lack of sleep due to his mind racing all night over the dangers of the day to come, Marshal stumbled into the kitchen and accepted the mug of coffee Shayna thrust into his hand. He breathed deep of the aromatic brew and sighed. Just what he needed to get started.

"Drink fast. You leave in fifteen minutes."

He glanced at the clock. Eight? "Why didn't someone wake me?"

"Castion said you tossed and turned all night. We thought you needed your sleep."

"No truer words ever spoken." He took a sip. True to her word, in exactly fifteen minutes, Pierce led Marshal and Payson through the trees and onto the street where Pierce called for a ride to pick them up.

"Keep your eyes open. We're vulnerable in the open."

Marshal nodded, anger at not having the chance to say goodbye to Kassy, racing through him. He'd caught a quick glimpse of her in a sparring match with one of Castion's men before Pierce whisked him away.

"Hold up." Rachel rushed to join them. "Shayna sent me to take my position as receptionist."

"You mean as a magic user in case we need one." Pierce grinned.

She smiled. "Of course. We can't let you simple men do things alone. Besides, Mary Ann says she's not interested in taking her job back now that she's gotten away from it. I'm capable of answering phones."

"We're glad to have you," Pierce said as a minivan pulled alongside them. He climbed into the front passenger seat, leaving the two back rows to the others.

Officer Charges met them at the back door. "Man, am I glad to hand the reins back to you guys. I never thought I'd say these words, but I miss patrolling the streets."

"Even with all the vampires?" Marshal patted his shoulder on the way to his desk in the bull pen.

"Yeah, even then. Things have stepped up, too. If not for the holy water around this place, we'd have been killed days ago."

Marshal stopped and faced him. "What do you

mean?"

"They keep testing the boundaries like wild animals in a cage. They're agitated. What happened?"

"We captured their leader," Pierce said, heading for his office.

"So this is almost over?" Charges glanced from Payson to Marshal.

"We're working on it. The women will be here in a couple of hours," Marshal said, "then me and one of them will be heading out to see what we can stir up."

"Alone?" The officer's eyes widened.

Marshal nodded. "We'll be fine. Have we lost any men?"

Sadness clouded his features. "Three. They're part of the group roaming the sidewalk."

"SWAT?"

"No losses, but those guys have protective gear."

Marshal headed for Pierce's office. "Charges said we lost three officers. The men need gear."

"Fetch the riot gear from the basement. No one leaves without it." Pierce riffled through the papers on his desk. "Charges is not a bookkeeper." A muscle ticked in his jaw. "He should have thought about the gear."

"You're back now to do the thinking." Marshal flashed a grin and headed for the basement. Despite what waited for them on the streets of New York, it felt good to be back.

He shoved open the door and stepped into the storage room, with barely time to lift his arm before a former uniformed officer sank its teeth into the armor he wore under his clothes. Since vampires could open doors, this one was smart enough to lie in wait, knowing someone would eventually enter the room.

Marshal shoved the undead against a wire cage and fought to pull his knife from its sheath on his belt. Succeeding, he plunged the dagger into its heart and stepped back.

The vampire turned to ash.

Marshal rolled up his sleeve, his blood running cold at the indentations in the sleeve of his armor. A few more minutes and the fangs would have punctured through. The vampires were growing stronger.

15

Kasdeya

"**What do you mean** they're getting stronger?" Kasdeya felt the chain mail under her clothes as she stared at the dents in Marshal's armor.

"This is not good." Deema paced the bull pen. "We don't have time to forge new armor for everyone from dragon scales, do we?"

"No." Shayna shook her head. "Agatha?"

"I can strengthen with a charm, but I'm not sure how long it will last. I might have to do the charm every day. That's a lot of work, and I'll not be left with enough strength to do anything else."

"If you can focus on that," Rachel said from the receptionist desk, "then the rest of us will work on potions and stuff. It's doable." She filed her nails with a brightly-colored emery board. "Sometimes you guys worry too much."

"You aren't the one who almost got bit!" Marshal's face darkened. "I could be trying to kill you right now."

"But you aren't." She stood. "Look, I have two children, children! Training to fight in a war no human child should ever see, much less experience. Don't talk to me about the dangers."

"Marshal and I are heading out there today with armor that isn't strong enough." Kasdeya choked back the mountain in her throat.

"I'll put a charm on the two of you right now," Agatha said. "Make sure to keep your necklace on and your protection around exposed body parts. Here." She tossed Kasdeya a red bandanna. "Make sure you wear this. I'm hoping you'll be making a lot of ash today." She laughed and raised her hands as Kasdeya tied the red strip of cloth around her neck. Silver rain fell upon her head, more frigid than any winter wind she'd ever experienced.

When Agatha finished with her, she turned and did the same to Marshal. "That's the best I can do. Don't dawdle. If you feel the cold leaving you, return here at once."

"Great." Marshal grabbed his gun holster from a hook near his desk. "We walk into the face of death feeling the breath of death itself breathing down our necks."

Despite the gravity of the situation, Kasdeya gave a nervous giggle. "The cold will remind us we're still alive."

"Good way of looking at things." Shayna's smile didn't erase the worry in her eyes. "Deema and I will be shadowing you. Be careful."

Kasdeya intended to. Their purpose was to find out where Alvar and his followers were hiding, not to engage them. Although, she knew they'd encounter some demons and vampires. She glanced up as the SWAT team entered and slipped her new rifle into the sling on her back.

"We're going to follow along on rooftops and in alleyways," the leader said. "We'll shoot if we have to, and hopefully keep the enemy from knowing the faeries are here. We heard they're to be incognito. You're in good hands, Detective, Ma'am."

Kasdeya glanced at Pierce who smiled. "Thank you."

"Got to keep my people as safe as possible. Go on now, before these guys are needed elsewhere." Pierce tossed Marshal a watch, then ducked into his office. "It's a walkie-talkie," he said, before closing the door.

Shayna sheathed her sword, as did Deema, and darted out the back door ahead of the SWAT team. Marshal took Kasdeya's hand and they followed.

The SWAT members darted in different directions, leaving Kasdeya and Marshal to head down the alley and avoid the undead crowd out front as much as possible. They stepped onto the street.

Kasdeya glanced left, then right, then left again. "I don't see any of the living."

"Eerie, isn't it? Pierce had a mandatory order given that no one is to be outside. If they have to go somewhere, they drive themselves or hail a cub. The subways are shut down."

She could barely comprehend the magnitude of

what it took to keep the city safe. The streets still moved with a few cars and undead. Demons darted here and there overhead, but the lack of conversation from people on cell phones sent a shiver down her spine that had nothing to do with Agatha's charm. "How are we to go out there unseen?"

"Carefully." He pulled her around the corner and as close to the building as possible. "Stay silent, move slowly," he whispered.

She shook her head. The undead weren't cats who relied on movement to spot their prey. They'd know the humans were there. Her heart told her they were walking into a trap. From the way Marshal kept stopping and listening, his gaze darting in every direction let her know he felt the same. She wanted to drag him back to the safety of the precinct. Being bait was a bad idea.

Marshal

This was a bad idea. Vampires turned to watch them pass, but none made a move to attack or stop them. Across the street, Marshal spotted a sniper, his rifle aimed on a vampire who stopped to watch Marshal and Kasdeya pass. He didn't like it one bit, so he yanked Kasdeya into the nearest alcove and shoved through the door of a drugstore.

"This is crazy," he said, glancing at the counter where a man in a white coat watched them.

"You two are nuts," the pharmacist said. "Can't you see what's out there? There's a curfew in place."

"We saw." Marshal stared through the glass.

Three vampires stared back, blocking the exit. His hunch was right. It was a trap, and he'd stepped right into it. "Find somewhere to hide," he told the man behind the counter. He turned the lock in the door. It wouldn't keep them out for long, but it might buy him and Kasdeya some time.

"Get away from the door," a voice came through the watch on his wrist. "I'm going to take them out."

Marshal and Kasdeya dove over the counter as shots rang out and the front door shattered. When he peered over the top, the three vampires were gone.

"Come on out, and hurry," the SWAT member said. "You've got another five coming fast. Tell the civilian to close shop and go home. Head east. We'll keep you posted."

Kasdeya stopped Marshal as he started to rise. "The penthouse where I once stayed. I bet that's where Alvar is hiding. It has top security and there's only one elevator and set of stairs to the top floor."

"Is it east?"

She nodded.

"Then let's go." Keeping her hand tightly in his, he led her at a sprint in the direction the team member had said. Turning to the left or the right as the man suggested got them to their destination without further incident, only to leave them with nowhere to hide. The front doors to the complex were locked.

"The fire escape?" Kasdeya motioned over their head. "It's the only way in. It'll take us to the second floor near a storage closet."

"Up you go." With his hands firmly planted against her red leather-clad bottom, he pushed upward as two vampires charged at them. Once she had a firm grip, he grabbed the bottom rung and swung himself up. "Hurry, darling. They're right on my heels."

He kicked, hitting one in the face and knocking it down. When they reached the landing, he pulled the ladder out of their reach. Another small act that would buy them a little time. Finding the window locked, he smashed it with the butt of his gun and rushed Kasdeya inside.

They exited into a small room full of cleaning supplies. Darting out, Marshal used one of the brooms to jam the knob into place.

"You're just there to get confirmation. Do not engage," said the voice through his watch. "Find him, and we'll take it from there."

"Great." How were they supposed to get out once they had confirmation?

Inching forward, they approached the elevator. "Where are the stairs?

"It's twenty stories up, Marshal."

"But safer than the elevator." He faced her. "We'll take the stairs. They can trap us there, but not cut the cables and send us plummeting."

She sighed. "Okay. It's down the hall to the right."

"Hold on, folks." The watch on Marshal's wrist crackled. "We've movement in the penthouse. Are we looking for a drop-dead, gorgeous brunette by any chance?"

"Radella." Kasdeya gripped Marshal's arm.

"Yes, and a large African American, and an ancient looking man in silver."

"Hold on." After a few seconds of silence, they received an affirmation. "I doubt I can get all three, but want me to take the shot? No need for you to go further. We've got the confirmation."

"Affirmative." Marshal raced back for the fire escape. Once the shot rang out, Alvar would know they were there, and his minions would swarm them.

A shot. "Got the big man."

"Kasdeya!" Alvar's scream ricocheted through the building.

The thick carpet muffled their footsteps. Marshal struggled to remove the broom, finally succeeded and earned himself a splinter in his palm for his effort. Pulling his gun, he shoved open the door and stepped back as Kasdeya removed the rifle from the sling on her back and took aim at the face in the storage-room window.

Her shot caught the male vampire in the face, knocking him from the ladder. She stuck out her arm to stop Marshal's forward progression. "I'll go first. The rifle will be better for picking them off the ladder. Be ready to move."

He grabbed her close and planted a hard, fast kiss on her lips. "Not the one I planned on giving you but had to get it in, in case…"

Smiling, she nodded and stepped up to the window. Shot after shot rang out until she faced him. "It's clear, but we'll have to hurry." She pulled her bandana to cover her mouth against the ash filling the air outside the window. "I'll come second to keep the coast clear for you, then you cover me while I climb down."

He gripped her hand. "Don't do anything stupid, Kassy. Don't go after Alvar alone."

"I won't. I promise."

Keeping his gaze on hers, he climbed out the window and onto the fire escape. One of the vampires had jumped high enough to pull the ladder back down, and he scurried to the ground as fast as could be done without falling. With his feet firmly on the ground, he stood with his back to the ladder, gun ready, and waited for Kasdeya to join him.

He breathed a sigh of relief as the ladder shook behind him. He'd harbored a fear she wouldn't keep her promise and almost sagged with relief when she did.

"Got you in my sights," the sniper said. "Three bogies coming fast on your right. Wait while I take them out, then go as fast as you can to the right. The SWAT van is waiting."

After they heard the three shots, Marshal and Kasdeya made a beeline for the van, leaping through the open door before it slammed shut behind them. A man in the driver's seat turned. "I'm Morgan. Glad to see you."

"Thanks for your help." Marshal grabbed Kasdeya in a hug. "We did it."

She smiled through her tears. "He'll leave again."

"No, we'll close off the building. He'll be as

trapped as he wanted us to be." He cupped her face. "You did great. You're capable of pushing aside your fear and doing what needs doing. Soon, you'll have no more reason to be afraid."

"There will always be evil in the world."

"Then, we'll travel to the ends of the earth fighting it together."

16

Kasdeya

They didn't make it two blocks before vampires surrounded the van. Morgan picked up the dash radio. "We need backup." He glanced over his shoulder and grinned. "We keep picking them off like this, and there might not be enough of them left for a final battle."

"We can only hope." Kasdeya glanced out the front windshield. Her heart stopped. More undead than she could count sprinted for the van. They did seem faster, stronger. "I think you'd better go."

Amidst shots raining down from the tops of buildings, the van surged forward, knocking the attackers to the side. From the shadows of an alley, Kasdeya spotted Shayna and Deema racing for the building where Alvar hid. Hot on their heels ran a large rottweiler. Agatha would make sure the traitor and his vampire whore stayed locked in place.

"You're on your own," said a voice on the radio. "We've got demons. We're surrounded, and it will take all we've got to fight them off. Stay safe."

Kasdeya stuck the barrel of her rifle out the window and started shooting with Marshal doing the same on the other side of the van. For every vampire that fell, two more took its place. Was there any living still in New York?

The van rocked as the horde and vehicle collided.

Kasdeya screamed and fell back.

Marshal gave her a quick glance but kept shooting. "All we have to do is make it to the precinct garage. Take the van all the way to the doors. We'll be able to get inside, but it will have to be quick."

"Yeah, but we'll be trapped," Morgan said.

"We'll worry about that when we have to. Floor it!"

The van careened ahead, swerving around a cab driving too slowly to escape the undead. They converged on the driver and his passengers.

Kasdeya aimed and fired, her bullets hitting the undead before they could break through the cab windows. She'd given those inside a chance. It would be up to them to make it further.

She swallowed back the bile that rose in her throat as it did every time she remembered her part in causing the destruction outside. She'd die before she ever forgave herself.

The van sped through the barrier blocking the precinct garage from anyone seeking free parking and skid to a halt in front of the door leading into the building. Marshal flung open the back door and shoved Kasdeya out. "Run."

She looked up to see demons swooping toward them. She didn't need to be told twice. With Marshal and Morgan flanking her, they ducked through the doorway and slammed the steel door closed. The demons and undead could go no further, thanks to Pierce's dousing the building with holy water. He'd covered the building well but hadn't had any left for the garage, nor the chance to have more water blessed. She leaned against the wall to catch her breath.

"I can't believe you two do this every day." Morgan wiped his perspiring forehead on the back of his hand, then grabbed the radio. "Everyone all right?"

"Yeah," someone answered, "but the street is swarming. We've no way to get free."

"Tell them to hold on." Marshal spoke into his watch, telling Pierce of the situation.

"We'll contact Shayna. We'll bring them back," Pierce answered.

By nightfall, with the help of Earin and a few other warriors, the entire SWAT team had been teleported to the precinct where everyone sat back to wait on Shayna and the others.

Shayna

Shayna stared up at the penthouse window, making out Alvar's figure as he looked down at them. Even with her good eyesight, he was too far away for her to read his expression. She didn't need to see him to know his anger and that he already plotted his escape and revenge.

Agatha reverted to her true form and set to work closing off all exits with magic and making sure the spell couldn't be broken even by Alvar. "The faerie is good," she said, "but I'm better. He'll stay up there and rot with Linc's body." The shape shifter's body splattered at their feet. "Or not. We need to get up there and seal that window."

"Can you do magic if you're two inches tall?" Shayna smiled and tilted her head. "I'll gladly give you a piggyback ride."

"I can do magic anywhere as long as I have two hands and not paws." Agatha handed her bag of tricks to Deema. "Guard this for me, will you?"

Shayna took the witch's hand. "*Shreank.*" They shrank to a diminutive size, and Agatha hopped on Shayna's back. "I'll try not to drop you."

"See that you don't. I hate heights." She wrapped her arms tight around Shayna's neck.

"Shift a bit or I can't flutter my wings."

Agatha muttered a complaint but complied. "Off with you."

Flying went slower with the extra burden, but a few minutes later they perched on the windowsill next to the window Alvar had pushed Linc out of. "Get busy, my friend." Shayna sat on the ledge, her legs hanging over the side and half-listened as Agatha paced, hands raised, and cast a shield across the windows.

"I knew there were pests out here. Too bad I've no lemon juice on hand."

Shayna turned just as Alvar struck her with a flyswatter. She fell, head over heels toward the ground below. The last sight she saw before landing in Deema's outstretched palm was Agatha's wide eyes.

"Are you all right?" Deema peered down at her with a worried look.

"I think I broke something. A lot of somethings. Put me down and go get Agatha before Alvar does."

Deema laid Shayna in the soft dirt of a potted plant and shrank, then flew to rescue their friend.

While she waited, Shayna breathed through the pain of multiple broken bones. She was alive because Deema had caught her. Landing on the sidewalk would have had her resembling nothing more than a stain on the concrete. But there were worse thoughts whirling through her mind than being knocked from the sky.

"I've got her." Deema reverted her and Agatha to normal size before wrapping Shayna's tiny form in her hand and teleporting them back to the precinct.

"What happened?" Pierce glanced down at Shayna's tiny form.

"Get back." Agatha placed her palm flat over Shayna. "You've enough power to revert back. Do it, so I can see what damage has been done."

Shayna screamed as agony ripped through her, stretching the broken bones as she turned to full size. Her breath came in gasps as she fought against the urge to vomit, pass out, or both.

"I'm only going to ask one more time." Pierce glared and crossed his arms. "What happened?"

"Alvar swatted her and she fell. Thanks to Deema, she isn't dead." Agatha shouldered him out of the way. "Healing is going to hurt more than the breaking, dear."

"Great." Shayna gritted her teeth and endured as Agatha touched every bone in her body, poking and prodding to find the broken ones. She gratefully accepted the sip of strengthening potion the witch held to her lips.

The others watched on as she screamed, cried, and gasped against the pain. Worse than having her blood drained and then replaced after the vampire bite, the healing seemed to take days rather than hours. By the time Agatha pronounced it done, Shayna was bathed in sweat. Faeries didn't sweat in her world. She hated the feeling.

"I need to get back to The Glen," she said, struggling to a sitting position. "Nurse Ida can take over from here."

"We'll all go." Pierce turned to Charges. "I'll be back tomorrow. The nights are yours."

The officer paled. "The nights are the worst."

"There's a curfew. If anyone is stupid enough to venture out, we can't help them. Only respond to domestic disputes and take SWAT with you. Do not answer any call that doesn't come from a legitimate complaint from a living person. We're only half an hour away." He handed Charges a watch similar to the one he and the other detectives wore. "Call me on this." He turned and took Shayna's hand. "We'll have you home soon, sweetheart."

She blinked up at him and nodded. "How about sooner?" They teleported, leaving Deema to bring the others.

She leaned heavily on Pierce's shoulder as they stepped through the portal. Once there, he scooped her into his arms and raced to the infirmary as her people crowded around them.

Nurse Ida met them at the door to the infirmary and ordered Pierce to lay Shayna on a bed. She gave her a quick check-over and nodded. "The witch does have skill. She's put you back together quite effectively." She pushed a cup of black liquid into Shayna's hands. "This will take away the pain but will taste horrible. Drink it all and keep it down."

Shayna forced back the bitter medicine, then lay flat against the pillows. "That was not an experience I want to repeat."

"Which one?" Pierce smiled and sat in the chair next to her.

"Any of it." She smiled. "Alvar is imprisoned with Radella. They might escape. I hope not, but for now we can concentrate on ridding the city of his monsters." She sighed. "No sign of the big man, Dan. I think he's busy turning people."

"He will become our top priority for now." Pierce took her hand and raised it to his lips, kissing her palm. "You still scare me to death at least once a day."

"I'll do better when this is all behind us," she said. "Alvar knows lemon juice kills us, Pierce."

He paled. "Then we'll find a way to protect you from it."

She nodded. "Stay with me while I sleep?"

"I wouldn't dream of going anywhere."

Marshal

Deema teleported Agatha, Kasdeya and him back to the house rather than to The Glen. Now, he sat on the sofa with Kassy snuggled into the crook of his arm, fast asleep.

Castion watched from a chair opposite the couch. "Sounds like a rough day."

"One of the worst. We almost didn't make it back."

The other man rubbed his chin. "I don't think it's smart for small groups to venture out. In my opinion, we need to focus on cleaning house. Get rid of as many of the monsters as we can. Venture out openly and fight every chance we get. Kill them faster than they can be created."

"I agree. Pierce called and said our first task will be finding the vampire Dan. Turned by Radella, he's quite the busy guy." He twirled a lock of Kassy's hair around his finger. "This woman is a marvel. Scared out of her wits until the actual fighting begins, then does what needs doing without a second thought."

"Aren't all warriors that way?"

Marshal nodded. "I think they are. What a strange world we live in now. I always thought I wanted to marry and start a family. Now, I'm not sure I want to bring a baby into all this."

"You can't stop living because things turn dark." Castion frowned.

Marshal shrugged. "I may be more scared than this woman sitting against me. It's easier when you don't have anyone you care about outside of the police force. You lose an officer, a partner, it rips at your heart but doesn't destroy you."

Castion nodded. "Instead of dwelling on the bad, why not look toward a hopeful future? If I've learned anything from Shayna, it's that there is always hope."

"You're softening, tough guy." Marshal laughed and stood, gently laying Kasdeya flat and covering her with a blanket.

"In all the right ways, I hope."

Marshal turned and thrust out his hand. "I'm glad to fight with you."

Castion returned his shake. "No more than I. Let's kick some evil butt and show we still have a world worth raising a family in."

17

Deema

"*How did he find* out?" Deema stared down at Shayna. "Alvar couldn't have known about our weakness to lemon juice without someone telling him."

"I'm missing one of my newer warriors." Earin rushed into the room.

Shayna swung her legs over the bed. "How is that possible?"

"He had to have gotten left behind when I teleported the SWAT team off the roof. In all the chaos, I missed him. Just as we took hands, a swarm of vampires converged on us." He knelt in front of her. "This is unforgiveable. I fear he's been captured."

"Get up." Shayna stood and moved to a chair. "It isn't unforgiveable, but it is irresponsible. Alvar will use this information to kill us all."

"What can he do?" Deema paced the floor. "He's locked up. No one can get in or out of that building. Unless he already has what he needs, we're safe, right?" Oh. "The demons can fly it to him."

Shayna grinned. "Let's go get some fire trucks."

They joined Pierce in the throne room where he studied a map of New York. He glanced up as they approached, his gaze locking on Shayna. "Should you be up?"

"I'm fine. We need you to find a priest and at least one fire truck. We have to douse Alvar's building."

He thought for a moment and nodded. "To keep the demons from giving him lemons."

She smiled. "Something like that."

"What if the hoses don't reach?" Deema asked. "Can you get a chopper in the air?"

"I don't know," Pierce said. "What if the demons bring it down?"

"We'll need a distraction." Earin joined them, his face grave. "I'll do it. It's my fault we're in this mess."

Deema whirled to face him. "We're in this together. You made a mistake. Move past it."

Clark put a restraining hand on her arm. "Let's not fight."

"Fine." She exhaled slowly. "Until this moment, we had an element of protection no one knew about. We have no defense against this."

"Agatha?"

She shook her head. "We can't have one drop touch us."

"An umbrella, then."

She paused her frantic pacing and glanced at Shayna. "That Agatha can do."

"Yes. We'll proceed with the holy water and have her put the same type of charm over us as she did with the acid rain." Shayna gathered her weapons. "Let's go."

They teleported to Kasdeya's property where the others were hard at work sparring. Deema and Shayna headed straight for the basement and Despair.

Deema stepped in front of the bars. "How did Alvar know about lemon juice? Don't pretend not to know. All your minds are linked somehow."

Despair laughed. "He caught himself a pretty little faerie boy. Don't worry. The faerie is out of his misery now. Radella took care of him."

Deema's blood ran cold. "She turned him?" She glanced at Shayna. "Is it possible?"

"I don't know. We've not run across this problem before. Dispose of Despair. He's a link we no longer need." She turned and marched away.

Without a word, Deema drew her sword and stabbed it through the bars, turning the demon to ash. She sheathed her weapon and joined the others outside.

Shayna stood on the porch, looking down as the others stared up at her. "Alvar captured and killed or turned one of the faeries. He now knows how to destroy us." She took a deep breath and exhaled slowly. "If he gets his hands on lemon juice—"

"Lemon juice?" Castion's brows raised. "As tough as you all are, mere lemon juice is your poison?"

Shayna nodded. "We don't like the word to get out, as I'm sure you understand, but now it can't be helped. We have no idea the effect on our warrior after being turned. He could be helpless or he could be the most powerful vampire this world has ever seen. Be prepared. We hit the streets in one hour."

Deema did her best to wet her dry mouth and failed. Things had gone from bad to worse in a matter of hours. She clenched her fists, wanting to kill Alvar with her bare hands…him and Radella. She could only hope she'd get her chance.

Alvar

Alvar tossed back a shot of whiskey and waited for the faerie to wake. Anxious to see the results of Radella's handywork he couldn't stand still. He paced back and forth in front of the window, occasionally pausing to look outside and revel in how he'd put Shayna in her place. Soon, he'd squash her with much more than a flyswatter. In fact, how wonderful would it be for Radella to turn not only the queen, but Deema and Kasdeya? Hell, why not the entire occupancy of The Glen? He'd control the most powerful army the world ever knew.

He laughed and did a little hop and skip back to the bedside.

Radella rolled her eyes. "You're like a child.

Hush now. Simon's waking."

The faerie's dark eyes opened. He hissed and lunged at Radella, hands outstretched. The chair under her broke, taking them both to the ground.

She shrieked and tried to remove his hands from her throat. "Help me," she wheezed.

Not exactly sure how he could stop a creature with such strength, Alvar lifted a lamp with a heavy crystal base and hit the faerie over the head. The lamp burst into shards. Rather than knocking the faerie unconscious, it turned its attention on Alvar.

Not good. He raced for the bathroom and slammed the door. "Kill that thing if you can't control him."

Radella cursed from the other side of the door.

From the sound of items breaking and the shaking of walls as bodies slammed into them, Alvar figured quite the battle raged. He cast a spell, putting a small hole in the door so he could see, and watched as Radella battled for her life.

Lesson learned. Turned faeries were not controllable and were extremely strong.

He sat on the edge of the tub and tried to come up with a spell that would destroy Simon. He'd removed all traces of silver from the penthouse weeks ago. He stared into the tub full of lemon juice. Would it still work on a turned faerie?

He opened the door and took cover behind it. "Throw him in the tub."

Radella darted for the bathroom.

Simon chased, skidding to a halt against the toilet. He bared his fangs and prepared to leap.

Radella two-hand shoved him into the tub big

enough for two.

Simon screamed as steam rose from the water. He writhed in agony, the flesh melting from his bones until the water looked more like chicken soup than a way to kill Shayna and the others.

Alvar leaned against the wall. "There goes our primary weapon down the drain." He laughed.

"Humor?" Radella glared. "He almost killed me. I've never seen such strength before and now he's gone. I will not turn another of your kind."

"Nor will I ask you to." An uncontrollable vampire was not something he wanted around. Lesson learned. He left the bathroom. "Close your door on the way out. It's starting to stink." Now, what could he use against the Light? Locked in the penthouse, neither Radella or himself would be of any use to anyone. The battle was over before it had begun.

"Stop pouting. I have a plan." Radella wiped a towel down her arm, removing all traces of Simon and the lemon juice. "No more relaxing here. I'm starving."

Kasdeya

Kasdeya stood on the sidewalk, rifle ready, and prepared to help the others protect two fire trucks from the demons and vampires who flew overhead and paced the opposite sidewalk. She laughed. They knew exactly what the priest who sat inside the cab meant.

Before leveling the hoses on the building, the firemen turned them full blast on the horde across the street. Kasdeya pulled her bandana over her nose and mouth as a cloud of ash rose. The firemen aimed the streams of water back to the building, soaking as high up as they could. Now that the immediate area had been cleared of demon and undead, a chopper flew overhead and dropped its load of water before flying off ahead of a new group of attackers.

"I don't see Simon," Shayna said, staring up at Alvar's window.

"Perhaps a faerie can't be turned." Kasdeya shrugged.

A sheet of paper fluttered toward them. Shayna reached up and snatched it from the air. "Let's make a deal," she read. "Let's you and me meet alone in a neutral place. Ah." She wadded up the paper. "The only place I want to see him is either dead in a grave or face-to-face in battle." She pointed at his window and shot a bolt of blue lightning as her answer. "We're finished here."

Firetrucks emptied, the rest loaded into the waiting SWAT van and headed back to the precinct. The team had cleared the garage earlier that morning, and Pierce had sprayed it with holy water to make sure it stayed clear of the enemy. They parked safely by the back door and trooped inside.

"Now what?" Kasdeya propped her rifle against the wall. "I'm getting tired of clearing the streets every day. We need to end this."

"I agree. We're going down the chain of

command." Shayna sat in a chair and propped her crossed feet on top of a desk. "With Alvar and Radella contained, we need to find Dan. Once he is eliminated, it's a matter of drawing the rest to a place of our choosing and destroying them. The dragons and giants will make short work of what's left."

"That's right." Deema perched on the corner of the desk. "Eliminate the magic users, then the muscle, and the rest will be easy."

"What about the faerie Alvar captured?" Kasdeya glanced from one face to the other. "Aren't you concerned for him?"

Shayna saddened. "I don't think he's alive. I only sensed two."

"Then fae can't be turned?"

Shayna shrugged. "We won't know for sure without seeing what happened to him. Let's not focus on what is done and cannot be changed. Where can we find Dan?"

Kasdeya sat in a chair opposite Radella. "He's the former bouncer of that strip club she used to manage, and I only met him a time or two. The man is duller than a spoon but big and strong. He preyed on women more than men and let the women he turned convert the men. I'm not sure where he would be, but concentrate on his attraction for the weaker sex." Even when human the man had taken women by force. She'd love to witness his destruction.

"We set a trap," Rachel said from her seat behind the reception desk. "I'll go, as long as you are watching to save me. It has to be someone he would perceive as weak,= and someone he doesn't know, which leaves out one of you three."

"I don't like it." Kasdeya shook her head. "I know I'm not the one in control here, but I'm the only one who knows what you'd be facing. No offense, Rachel, but he'll only attack someone younger and more beautiful, except to feed. He's less picky then."

Rachel narrowed her eyes. "So I'm no good for anything other than food?"

"Sorry." She gave a wry grin.

Shayna leaned back in her chair and stared at the ceiling. "It has to be someone who can help protect themselves." She set her chair down with a thump. "You, Kasdeya."

"But he knows me."

"Yes, and you'll be a prize he can't resist. If he's as dumb as you say he is, and with Alvar and Radella not able to give him orders, he'll act on his own. He'll be reckless and impulsive."

Kasdeya nodded. "You're right. He won't be able to resist the temptation of converting me." And...she was bait...again.

18
Kasdeya

Kasdeya left her rifle in Marshal's protection. Today's task would require hand-to-hand combat if she got unlucky. Got? She'd been unlucky since the day she met the pastor over a hundred years ago. So long ago, she'd forgotten his name, just not what his actions had caused.

Her boots thudded dully on the sidewalk as she made her way to Central Park. The emptiness of the city sent shivers up and down her arms causing the hairs to stand on end. Shayna had chosen the park because of its size and tree cover, thus allowing her and the others to have better camouflage.

Taking a deep breath, Kasdeya set off down a popular jogging trail, doing her best to look as if she were the hunter rather than the prey. She'd skipped breakfast and now her stomach rolled. Her gaze searched the trees, although she doubted Dan's attack would be subtle. He seemed more like the type to enjoy toying with his dinner.

The eerie silence of the park pricked at her nerves until each one twanged. "I don't see anyone," she whispered in her earpiece. "Not even a homeless person."

"They've all been turned. If you see anything moving in the park, it is not friendly," Marshal answered. "You're doing great, sweetheart."

Easy for him to say. She fought to keep her steps slow and steady despite the urge to sprint down the path and away from the encroaching danger. Her lungs squeezed, and she pulled her inhaler from her pocket. She took a deep puff and put it away. Her heart still raced, but there was no quick fix for fear.

A twig snapped to her right. She whirled, sword in hand as Dan stepped from the trees.

"Hello, gorgeous." He glanced up and down the path. "Why are you out here all alone?" He grinned and licked his lips. "It's getting harder and harder to find food, but then you aren't food, are you? What a prize you'll be."

"Stay back." She stepped back until a tree trunk stopped her. Why hadn't Shayna come to her aid yet? "I'm going to kill you, Dan. You are most definitely *not* a prize, except for maybe a booby prize."

"You're going to kill me while being human again?" He tilted his head as if she'd said something foreign. "Maybe you had the strength once, but no more. This will be fun. I'll turn you slowly. Maybe you'll enjoy it as much as I will."

"Hold fast," Marshal said. "We don't want him to get away. Once he engages, the rest of us will join you."

Kasdeya groaned. Perspiration soaked the shirt under her leather jacket. "Well, come on then. I don't have all day."

"I have eternity." Dan laughed and continued to move toward her.

"Famous last words." She tried leaping to the side when he lunged, but the man's speed was too much for her. She tripped over an exposed tree root and fell flat on her back.

Dan bent over her and bared his fangs. "I like it when they resist."

A sword protruded through his chest. His eyes widened as he glanced down at the silver blade. He cursed and turned to ash.

Shayna held down a hand to help Kasdeya to her feet. "Well done. You sufficiently distracted him."

"Too close for my comfort." She brushed the ash from her clothes. "Now what?"

"We drag out Agatha's crystal ball and lure Alvar to the mountains. We're going to end this now."

Rather than head back to the precinct, they went home where Castion and the others waited to hear the outcome of Kasdeya's encounter with Dan. Thank the Light, it had turned out well.

Agatha poured mugs of coffee and passed them around. "Since Kasdeya still walks and breaths, I assume Dan is gone?"

"Into the wind." Kasdeya grinned and accepted

a mug. Her gaze met Marshal's warm one. She lived to spend another day with him.

Marshal

Marshal could breathe again. His heart had been lodged in his throat the entire time Kasdeya stood on the park's path alone. When Dan had stepped out to meet her, he'd almost thrown up. The urge to go to her aid and not being able to had eaten at him like the lemon juice the faeries feared.

"I rather like our odds now," he said, raising a toast to the woman he loved. "The demons and vampires are without a leader. They'll scatter on the battlefield when they see us coming."

"That's the plan." Deema leaned against the counter. "Yet, it seems too easy somehow."

"Easy?" Kasdeya's brow furrowed. "You weren't in the park alone."

"Neither were you."

"Well, it seemed like I was." Kasdeya sat in a chair next to Marshal. "I don't want to be bait again. Twice is two times too many."

"I'm proud of you," Shayna said. "When you made the choice to join us, you never looked back. Maybe your original reason was for selfish means, but since Alvar is out of commission and yet you stay, I believe you are here now for the right reasons."

Kasdeya glanced up at Marshal. "I have one

important reason to stay."

Standing, he took her by the hand and led her to the front porch away from prying eyes. "I think it's time I gave you a proper kiss, Kassy."

"Aren't I the one who promised you a kiss?" She smiled, her dark eyes twinkling.

"Then, we'll kiss each other." He lowered his head and pressed his lips to hers. What started soft and sweet soon turned heavier and more demanding until his breath left his lungs. He stepped back and rested his forehead against hers. "Marry me, Kassandra Brown." Such an ordinary name for an anything-but-ordinary woman. "Become Kassandra Marshal."

She stiffened in his arms. "There is still a battle to be fought, Luke. One of us might die."

"We might, but we can live the time we have left as husband and wife."

"Where would we find someone to marry us? Most of the city is in hiding."

His heart leaped. She was actually considering his proposal rather than giving him an outright no. "We'll find one. I don't care if we say our vows here, alone, or with the others as witnesses. Your pledge is enough for me." His hands slipped down her arms to join hands with hers. "Is it a yes?"

"I want to say yes, with everything in me, Luke. My heart soars at your proposal, but my head says now is not the time. Can't you just love me for now, and we'll discuss this again after the war is fought?" Tears shimmered in her eyes.

His heart sank. Lies teased at his brain saying she only put up with him because she needed him.

That she'd vanish once she'd had her revenge. Without another word, he jumped off the porch and headed for the clump of trees behind the property.

Being careful to stay inside the shield, he sat on a plot of grass beside a stream. He'd been foolish enough to believe she loved him. Had those words actually ever left her lips? He couldn't remember. What an idiot. Blinded by her beauty and an inner goodness he started to think he'd only imagined.

Human love was nothing like what Shayna and Pierce shared. A vow, a pledge, a physical act bound them together for life. Here, he needed vows before a preacher from a woman who believed the words she spoke. It hurt to think Kasdeya might not be that woman.

"Luke?"

He refused to turn and give her the satisfaction of his emotions written across his face. "What?"

"I'd like to help you understand how I feel. Will you listen?"

"I'll listen, but I can't promise to believe what you say."

She sat on the ground a couple feet away and picked up a rock a little smaller than her palm. She tossed it up and down a few times before casting it into the creek. "I came from a family where a nanny raised me. A kind woman, but she wasn't my mother. Then, I fancied myself in love with a man, and we know how that turned out. I don't think I know what love is, Luke."

"And you won't let me show you."

"You are showing me, I think." She put a hand on his arm.

He fought the urge to jerk away. "I don't know what to think anymore. I thought we had something special, you and I."

"We do. Would you look at me?"

He sighed and faced her.

"You already consume my every thought," she said, her words soft. "If we wed, pledge, whatever you want to call it, you'll fill even more of me, and me of you. We won't give the battle everything we have. I no longer want to die on the battlefield. I want to live and spend my life with you." She stood. "That will have to be enough for now." She turned and walked away.

Marshal jumped to his feet and chased after her. Putting his hands on her shoulders, he spun her to face him. "It is enough." He pulled her close and kissed her until both of them were breathless.

Radella

Radella's gaze settled on Alvar at the window. The time had come to make the move she'd been planning for weeks. With Abaddon in chains, Alvar was the only thing standing between her and complete power. "Come to bed, Alvar. We've no other way to spend our time."

He turned with a smile, his ancient face more wrinkled than ever. The once-handsome faerie now looked like a defender of hell, filled with as much evil as Radella. But he had one thing she didn't have and that was magic.

She patted the mattress. "What are you waiting for?"

Still grinning, having no idea what awaited him, he slipped into the bed beside her. Radella climbed on top of him, bared her fangs, and sunk them into his neck. He was no match for her strength. She sucked, feeling his power and magic course through her. When he lay still, she wiped his blood from her lips and climbed from the bed.

She dressed in her customary black leather shirt and pants. The time had come to see whether her plan had worked or whether she'd spend eternity alone in the penthouse. She packed a backpack with the things she'd need, then climbed onto the windowsill, and jumped.

She fell straight to the pavement below, landing on her feet. The sidewalk crumbled under the weight of her. She raised her hands and shot out a streetlamp. A laugh burst from her, scattering pigeons who sought crumbs under a tree.

She was now the most powerful being in this world and the next.

19

Radella

Radella approached the police station just after dark. The holy water would have no effect on her. She wasn't a demon, but she now ruled them. If she could find a way into The Glen, she'd convert a handful of faeries and control the outcome of the war. She wouldn't make the same mistake as she had with Simon. The newly turned would remain chained until he or she learned to obey.

There was the one she sought. She ducked behind a squad car in the parking garage and waited until Officer Charges moved close enough for her to pounce.

He spun, gun in hand, as she leaped but not soon enough. She clobbered him alongside the head, then tossed his unconscious body over her shoulder. Humming a happy tune, she strolled from the garage and toward a set of vacant warehouses a few blocks away. She dumped the officer in a corner of the room and waited.

After an hour, he groaned and sat up. Fear flamed in his eyes as his gaze landed on hers. "What do you want with me?"

"Entry." She'd spent the time he'd slept devising a way to make him talk. She didn't believe he'd do so for his own life, so she'd gone back to the station and taken another. The rookie officer, tied and gagged at her feet, whimpered. "Tell me where the portal to The Glen is or I will turn this man."

Charges frowned. "You can't enter without an invite, and I can't give you that."

Damn. She hadn't known that little fact. When she'd been there before, she'd been taken as a prisoner. She shrugged. "Then I have no need for either of you." She sank her teeth into first the rookie, then Charges, not draining them of all their blood, but taking enough to satisfy her hunger and turn them. Let the chief of police face his own men on the field. She'd devise another plan to thwart Shayna.

Kasdeya

Kasdeya slept as if she'd not for days and woke warm in the knowledge that Luke loved her enough to wait for her to make up her fickle mind. She knew what she wanted, and it was him, but after the war when they were free to do as they pleased. Then she'd marry him gladly. Nothing big. A small ceremony surrounded by their friends in The Glen if Shayna would allow. If not for the faeries, they'd never have met and she wanted their union to be perfect in every way.

She made her way to the kitchen, not surprised to see Earin and Becky, heads together in private conversation. The two were almost inseparable now. She smiled. A faerie and a witch. Who could have guessed?

They weren't the only two in deep conversation. On the back porch, Shayna and Pierce, their faces creased with worry, glanced up as she entered.

"What's wrong?" Kasdeya's steps faltered.

"Officer Charges and a rookie have gone missing," Pierce said. "I'm headed back to the precinct with Payson and Marshal."

"To do what?"

"Find them alive, I hope." He gave Shayna a quick kiss. "I'll see you later?"

"Right after training," she said.

"I'd like to go now." Kasdeya glanced from one to the other. "We don't need more training. We need to keep on the offensive."

"Listen to you speaking the lingo." Marshal approached her from behind and kissed the back of her neck. "I agree. The action is in the city. We need to go there. We can house operations in the garage now instead of here. It's two stories high, so there's plenty of room."

Shayna thought for a moment. "All right. I'll

gather up Agatha and the others and meet you there. It's time to contact Alvar."

By noon, they'd gathered at the station and Agatha had placed a charm to keep others, dead or alive, from entering the garage. Kasdeya trooped into the station with the others and watched as Rachel blocked the back and front doors. From now on, the only way in or out would be through the garage or teleportation.

Marshal had cut a few holes in the wall to allow the barrel of a gun to aim through, but nothing else gave access to the front or back.

Paddy, Seamus and a few dozen leprechauns had joined them along with Ennis and his company of gnomes. Fighting in Ireland had slowed down to nothing the few giants there couldn't control. Olga and the dragons waited to be summoned. The fight had come to New York in earnest.

Kasdeya stood in front of the double-glass front doors. "Pierce, you need to come here." Outside, glaring in at them stood Officer Charges and a rookie, both with fangs bared.

"Oh, no." Pierce's face darkened. "I have to kill them, my own men, men I trained myself. Officer Charges had been a good cop. One of the best."

"I'll do it." Payson stepped up beside him. He aimed his pistol and pulled the trigger, taking out the rookie first, before turning the gun on Charges. "I'm sorry, friend."

Kasdeya jerked as the gun went off and the officer fell. Saddened, Pierce and Payson turned away from the window. Unfortunately, the two wouldn't be the last casualties of this war.

The mood in the place turned morose. No one spoke, each deep in their thoughts.

Rachel sat behind the receptionist desk, wiping away tears on a tissue. The phone rarely rang anymore as even the thugs stayed inside or became part of the undead. The city had fallen. All they could hope to do was save the rest of the world.

Kasdeya went in search of Marshal, needing to be with the one person who made her feel as if everything would be all right. She found him staring at a map of the city with the SWAT team leader, Harry Dodge, she thought she'd overheard someone say.

"This area is pretty clear of people." Dodge pointed to a spot near the Canadian border. "Your dragons will make a big mess of the scenery, but trees will grow back. People won't."

Shayna plopped a cloth-covered crystal ball in the center of the map, and circled the area Hodge had pointed out. She removed the covering and peered into the ball. "Alvar."

"Is no longer here." Radella's cruelly beautiful face sneered back at them. "I disposed of the old man and took what power from him I could. So, where are we meeting, my sweet faerie?"

Shayna glanced up at the others, her eyes wide.

Kasdeya's legs weakened. An already powerful evil had become more so. She'd be turning what humans she could find at a greater speed. Who knew exactly what she was capable of now? Kasdeya was pretty sure they were facing an unprecedented event.

"Look at the map," Shayna said. "Surely you

can read one, being so powerful now."

Radella's gaze flicked to the map under the ball. "Ah, trying to keep people safe? You won't win this. Soon, I'll own this entire world, and when I do, I'll take yours as well and keep you as my pretty little pet in a jar. As for Kasdeya, she won't live long enough to worry about anything."

"You can try, Radella, but I still know way too much about you." Kasdeya peered into the ball, pushing down the fear rising in her throat. "See you on the battlefield."

"With pleasure, you miserable human."

Shayna placed the covering back on the ball and set it far enough away Radella couldn't hear them. "This is not good."

"How much power could she have gotten from Alvar?" Kasdeya asked.

"Any is too much for one such as her."

Shayna

Needing more wisdom than she possessed, Shayna headed for The Glen, alone, and summoned Gorna. Brigette might be the only one with any knowledge of the power Radella might now possess. Having exiled herself to the woods and cabin where Agatha had once lived, she no longer wanted any part in the coming war. Not after the death of Linette, but Shayna would insist on the former queen's help.

Rather than spend the day traipsing through the thick forest, she circled the woods on Gorna's back until they found a small clearing large enough for the dragon to land. "Wait for me," Shayna said, patting the dragon's back.

"I'll be here." Gorna laid her massive head on her feet and closed her eyes.

Shayna sprinted between the trees until she reached the cottage. Smoke rose from the chimney. Good. Brigette was home. She stepped forward and knocked. When no one answered, she pushed the door open and peered inside.

Brigette glanced up from where she sat reading a book. "Come in." She sighed and stuck a peacock feather between the pages as a bookmark. "I will not join the fight, Shayna. I don't have the heart for it."

"I'm here to ask for information." She sat across from the beautiful, dark-haired faerie. "Although I don't understand your decision not to fight, I respect it."

"What information do you seek?"

"Radella killed Alvar and said she now has his power. Is that possible?"

Brigette paled. "To some degree, yes, although she cannot possess all he once had, nor can she know his spells. Those were learned."

"How dangerous is she?" Shayna leaned forward, balancing her arms on her knees.

"Extremely. I'm not sure how adverse to silver she will be now. Although it can harm her, I don't know if it will kill her." Bridgette fiddled with the sleeve of her robe. "She will have some skill with magic, bolts of lightning perhaps. She'll be stronger and faster."

"Can she fly?"

Brigette shrugged. "All of this is speculation. It's never happened before." She leaned back in her chair. "I'm not sad Alvar is dead."

"I don't think anyone is. The other vampires are also faster, but this happened before Alvar's death."

"Alvar found a way, just as he found a way to create his new breed of demons. The coming battle will be fierce, my friend. You need to prepare. Come." She stood and led Shayna through a trapdoor in the floor of the cottage.

They descended a flight of rickety wooden stairs. Brigette lit a lantern and held it over a table of assorted items. "I may not wish for combat, but I have not been entirely idle while here." She picked up a willow stick. "An old-fashioned wand with the power of the ancient witches. Give this to Agatha. She's the only one whose magic is powerful enough to use it." She removed a quiver of arrows from a hook on the wall. "For Hanna, imbued with magic. Even if her aim is off, these arrows will strike the nearest follower of the dark. And for you, my queen, I give you my crown."

She opened the lid of a carved gold chest and withdrew a crown of rubies, emeralds, and sapphires set into gold. "This will protect you from lemon juice, demon spit, vampire bite, you name it. Once placed upon your head, it cannot be removed unless you command it to let go."

Shayna bowed her head as Brigette placed the crown on her head. "What about my people?"

Brigette's eyes saddened. "You must face Radella alone, queen to evil leader. The others will fight the battle, but you must confront the vampire alone." She cupped Shayna's cheek. "She will target Kasdeya first. Wait until she makes the attempt, then step in. Send Kasdeya to the safety of the others and finish Radella."

"If I perish?" Shayna's heart rate increased.

"You will not. I cannot say the same for the others. You will lose people precious to you. Prepare your heart. Do not despair. No one is entering the fight unaware of the perils."

"I know, but they follow me, sharing my hope we will win the war."

"You will win." Brigette gave a sad smile. "But not everyone will survive."

Tears blurred Shayna's vision. "Do you know who will die?"

"I have seen who will fall if you take too long to finish Radella." She handed Shayna the silver, jewel-handled dagger from her belt. "Plunge this into Radella's heart. Once she is dead, the others will also die."

"All of them?" Shayna stared at the knife.

Brigette chuckled. "Only those at the battle. There will still be evil to hunt down, but your job will be done. The sooner you kill her, the sooner the war ends and your friends' lives will no longer be in danger. Go in the Light, Shayna. I wish you well."

"You possess more power than I ever imagined." Shayna glanced around the dirt room.

"Linette and I started work on these items the moment we reconciled. She would be proud of you."

Shayna took a deep breath and released it slowly. With a nod, she whirled around and left, there being nothing more to say.

20

Shayna

Shayna headed back to The Glen and rallied her troops there. Eyes widened, knees bent, as she passed with the crown on her head. They all knew she wore no ordinary crown. The one she'd received upon Linette's death lay protected in a velvet box deep in Gorna's cave. No, this one sparkled with power, lifting the ends of her hair with electricity.

Shayna acknowledged their reference with a nod but no joy. How could she be happy knowing people she loved would die within the week, for she'd made up her mind the time had come to end the fight.

The leprechauns, sprites, faeries, giants, and dragons came at her call. She gave the order for them to wait for her on the top of Mount Marcy, the tallest mountain in the state of New York. Once they had gone on their way, she took the faerie warriors, Logan and Hanna, to the police station's parking garage.

Rachel pulled her children into a tight hug, then stepped back as Shayna handed Hanna the quiver of arrows. She folded her hands in front of her as tears rolled down her face.

Shayna explained the magic of the arrows. "You are not to step foot on the field, child," she said. "Logan will be beside you to protect you with his sword." Brigette's words of doom would not lessen Shayna's attempt at keeping her people, her family, safe. She went on to tell them of the crown she wore, leaving out that some of those in the garage would die. "The other races fighting with us are waiting on the battlefield."

"Our job now is to get Radella and her followers there," Pierce said. From the concerned look on his face, Shayna knew he knew she wasn't telling them everything of her visit with Brigette. She'd decided only to tell her inner circle, not the entire group. "Pack up everything you need. We leave at nightfall."

When most of the fighters had left, she turned to those remaining. "Brigette said I must face Radella alone when she confronts Kasdeya. The fight will end the moment I plunge this dagger into her heart."

"Then do that first thing," Kasdeya said, her voice shrill with stress. "Hunt her out now and finish her off."

"She won't emerge until the fight. I'm sorry, Kasdeya, but once again we need you as bait." Shayna glanced around the circle. "Brigette told me that many will die. She wouldn't tell me who, and I will do everything in my power to make sure you are not one of the fallen."

"That's war, isn't it?" Castion glanced around the group. "Death and destruction?"

Deema, face grim, nodded. "It doesn't make the loss any easier."

"I'm not saying it does. I've lost men in the past. It rips away a piece of your heart every time." He looked resigned. "I've got to prepare my men. I'll meet you here later." He whirled and marched away.

"Did Brigette see the outcome of the war?" Pierce asked.

"Yes. We win." Shayna sagged against the nearest car. "How many lives we lose depends on how fast I can kill the much-faster, much-stronger, magic-wielding Radella."

"Let's hope you're still stronger than she." Kasdeya moved closer to Marshal. "I don't like being bait."

"Other than me," Shayna said, "you're the one she hates the most. I'd take your place if I could, but Brigette said it must be you." She motioned Agatha close and asked her to set the crystal ball on the hood of the car.

Agatha removed the cloth and stepped back. "I sure wish there was a way to trap that fiend inside this ball."

Shayna couldn't agree more. "Radella."

"Oh, nice crown." The vampire sneered. "I wish you hadn't killed Dan. Having to do the majority of turning on my own is quite wearing."

"Boo hoo," Agatha muttered.

"You'll be the third person I kill, witch."

"I'm waiting."

"Hush." Shayna narrowed her eyes. "We will meet you at day break on Mount Marcy in three days' time. Make sure you're there."

"That's an invitation I can't refuse." She disappeared.

"We need to make our game plans." Deema locked gazes with Shayna.

"I'm sending the witches ahead of us to set up camp. When we join them, we'll gather in my tent and come up with our best plan. For now, get some rest." Shayna headed for Pierce's office, the only room with any semblance of privacy other than the restroom.

Pierce followed her, closed the door to his office, then pulled her into his arms. "We'll work together to minimize casualties."

"I know." She leaned against his chest and cried.

Kasdeya

Bait again. Lucky her. Kasdeya checked and double checked her armor and weapons. This had to be her punishment for her past crimes. Fitting, really. She smiled though, remembering the secret conversation she'd had with Gorna. The dragon promised to let Kasdeya witness the end of

Abaddon. She had to live long enough to see it through. Then, if the Light was with her, she'd move into a future with Marshal.

"Are you okay?" Marshal stepped into the breakroom to join her.

"I can't wait until this is all over."

"Try not to die on me, okay?" He gave her a crooked smile that sent her heart tumbling.

"I'll do my best. Make sure you do the same." Her returned smile trembled.

"I don't plan on dying for a long time, sweetheart." He held his arms open. "It's time to go."

"We've time. It will take the faeries a while to teleport everyone. I'm in no hurry." She stepped into his hug.

"Well, I am. The sooner we get there, the sooner this all ends, and you can answer my question of marrying me."

"You're such an idiot." She laughed. "You have more to worry about than an answer you already know."

"I want you to say the words, Kassy." He gave her a quick kiss, then led her to the garage where a group of nervous people gathered, waiting their turn to leave.

Castion and his men counted ammo and checked guns, sharpened knives, anything to keep their hands busy. Kasdeya didn't blame them. Hadn't she done the same thing over and over until there was nothing left to check?

As she took Deema's hand, she took one last glance at the street outside the police station and hoped she'd see it again in the light without undead patrolling the sidewalk.

They landed next to a large tent the same shade of green as the grass. Away from the camp, Agatha and the witches worked on constructing several towers placed behind the line of battle for the archers and other long-range fighters to stand on. Further out, the gnomes dropped boulders over and over, making a deep trench between the camp and the field.

What would be Kasdeya's part in the preparations? Sit back and wait to face Radella, then run like a frightened child when Shayna appeared? She didn't like that plan. Still, the others knew more about fighting than she did. Like it or not, she'd follow orders.

She parted the tent flap and stepped inside. She froze at the sight of Abaddon in chains behind bars in a corner of the tent.

He glared in her direction, no longer the powerful leader of the undead he'd been the last time she'd seen him. Now, he'd wasted away to a fraction of his former self, skinny and unwashed.

"What is he doing here?" She glanced at Shayna.

"With the dragons here, he had to come. We cannot leave him unguarded." Shayna cut her a look. "Gorna said you had unfinished business with him."

"For after the battle." Kasdeya plopped into a chair. "Won't he hear our planning and find a way to tell?"

"No. Agatha made him deaf. She enjoyed the

task a little too much." Shayna turned back to a map spread out on the table.

Kasdeya didn't ask how the witch had accomplished the task. From the defeated look on Abaddon's features, it had involved torture.

She'd see enough gruesome acts in the next few days to last her a long time. How far she'd come from her former evil self. Then she'd relished violence; now she abhorred it. Shayna and her people really did have a good effect on those that hung around them long enough.

She drummed her fingers on the arm of her chair and stared at Abaddon, smiling. Oh, if he only knew his fate in a few days. Gorna promised to make it quick with no bloodshed.

"What has you looking so chipper?" Deema's brow creased. "Are you looking forward to the fight?"

"Nope. Just what comes after."

Deema glanced at the cage. "You've something diabolical up your sleeve."

"I sure do." The laugh she'd been holding in escaped her. Okay, maybe she'd gone a little crazy with all that was going on, but looking forward to Abaddon being dealt with once and for all would get her through the next few days.

"I don't like it," Shayna said. "But I don't fault you."

"Stop reading my mind." Kasdeya groaned.

"Then stop thinking so loud."

"Are you going to stop me?"

"No."

The others watched the conversation with

confusion. Deema shrugged and disappeared outside with the excuse of supervising the training exercises.

Kasdeya sighed and followed. She might as well work on her endurance. She still tired before any of the others.

Radella

Radella swiped the blood from her lips with the back of her hand. She'd sent others out to recruit, still others to find shifters willing to fight on their side, and still she didn't think they'd have enough fighters. Without Alvar around to create more of his super-size demons, even they had dwindled in numbers, thanks to the detective's idea of dousing them with holy water.

She stared at those she had to work with. Not enough to fill Central Park. With the larger number fighting alongside Shayna, Radella would have to kill the queen quickly. Maybe she should focus on her death first, rather than Kasdeya's. Then, when they were all dead, she'd release Abaddon from his chains and rule at his side forever.

Pointing at the top of a tree, she sliced it in two with a blast from her fingertips. It took too much concentration before the lightning would strike. She hadn't taken enough of Alvar's power. She couldn't fly no matter how hard she tried and none of the demons would act as a ride for her.

She approached a cluster of them reclining under the branches of an oak. "Three of you go and bring me back word of our enemy. We need to know the numbers we're up against."

Three of the smaller ones took to the skies, flying away like crows. Radella sent out five vampires to turn as many as possible in a day's time, a task that grew harder as humans stayed inside. Still, they'd find a few foolish enough to venture outside in search of food.

She glanced at the dark streetlamps. The idea to shut down the power stations had been brilliant. Food wasted, pipes devoid of running water. People were forced to venture out at some point, but too many of them had prepared in advance, thanks to the chief of police. He'd be the fourth she killed. Or maybe she'd keep him as a plaything. He was pretty enough.

From the first time they'd met, she wanted him. Not having a man trip over himself at the sight of her had piqued her interest immediately. Not only with him, but with the other two detectives as well. What did they see in the faeries? Radella's beauty outshone them all.

She'd be the most beautiful and terrifying ruler the world had ever had the misfortune of bowing before. She laughed, the sound ringing through the silent night.

21

Kasdeya

Kasdeya stood on a small hill overseeing the camp and watched as those she'd fight alongside woke and started their day. How many would die? She glanced overhead where the dragons circled. Shayna had said she'd speak to them after breakfast and lay out the battle plans so each knew their part and could train accordingly. She did her best to count heads. A hundred. One hundred souls stood against an evil that wanted to claim both her world and the fae's. It didn't seem near enough.

Training was nothing more than a façade. Once the battle began, it would be a fight-or-die scenario. She eyed the trenches. The vampires could not fly, but the demons could, the wily creatures who whispered lies and words of despair. Words that pierced the heart the same as silver-tipped arrows.

She sighed and headed for the camp as Shayna climbed one of the towers.

She held up her hands for the crowd to quiet. The morning sun struck the crown on her head, sending rays of gold over them all. Impressive, but it didn't foster a lot of hope in Kasdeya. How could a head accessory help anyone other than the one who wore it?

"My friends," Shayna began. "I met with Queen Brigette yesterday, and she has seen the outcome of this war. We will win."

Cheers rose into the morning air.

"But we will suffer casualties." Shayna paused, her gaze sweeping over them. "I don't know how many, and I will do all I can to lessen the number. I must defeat Radella to stop the battle and will do so as fast as possible. I ask that you fight with caution, relying on the skills you possess to protect not only yourselves but the one fighting beside you. The trenches will stop the coming horde, but I don't know for how long. The vampires are faster and stronger than the last time we fought."

Way to instill confidence. Kasdeya crossed her arms.

"While the enemy tries to find a way across the trenches," Shayna said, "The dragons will fly overhead, breathing down fire. Once the enemy is within range, our archers and magic users will take down those they can. Then it becomes hand-to-hand combat. Be ready, be strong, and know that we will emerge victorious!"

Despite her dire words that some would perish, more shouts and cheers rose. Kasdeya grimaced and turned away. Her gaze fell on Marshal. He seemed focused on her rather than their leader. Kasdeya would gladly meet the enemy alone if it would guarantee his safety. But nothing she could do would guarantee the thing she wanted most…a life with Marshal.

She retrieved her rifle from the tent she shared with several female faerie warriors and headed to the plot of grass used as target practice. After letting herself be used as bait, she was to return here and become part of the first line of defense. She'd rather just plunge her sword into Radella's heart and be done with it all.

"You killing Radella will not stop the war." She hadn't heard Shayna approach. "Only the one who wears this crown can do that. You would kill her, yes, but the others would not fall. This is how it must be."

Kasdeya faced her. "I know, but I don't have to like the plan."

"You won't die by Radella's hand."

"That's good to know." She faced the target, a crude drawing of a vampire, aimed, and squeezed the trigger. A hole appeared right where a heart would beat. When she turned, Shayna had disappeared.

Despite her sour feelings toward what had to transpire, Kasdeya did not envy the queen's position. A lot rode on her strong shoulders. Her bright blue eyes were shadowed more than not. Sorrow lined her face. No, she did not want to trade places with Shayna and be the one to give orders that would send some to their deaths.

"Good shot," Marshal said, taking a place beside her. He raised a rifle and aimed, his shot landing in the shoulder of the drawing. "Not a kill shot."

"I'll be on the tower, Luke." She gripped his arm. "Please promise me you won't die."

His shoulders sagged. "I can't promise that. I'll be in the middle of the fight, but it's good to know you'll be up out of harm's way."

"There is no safe place. The demons have wings." And she feared what they would whisper as they flew around her head. She may have gained physical strength during her training, but her mental state was untested.

Shayna

"We will have the tunnels dug in time," Ennis said. "The gnomes will attack from underground once the trench has been breached."

"The leprechauns are ready," Paddy added, "although our power is not as strong as other races, we are mighty fighters." He whipped off a peaky hat from his head. "Stole something from the old days. Razor blades in the brim. Blinding them might give us enough time to stick a knife in 'em."

Shayna nodded. "Olga said the giants will be part of the first wave. They can take out several vampires in one swoop and hopefully distract the others from those of us on this side of the trench."

Plans were falling into place, igniting a small flicker of hope in her chest.

Brigette's words had threatened to snuff the flame out, but she hadn't known the full scope of those following the Light into battle. It would be enough. It had to be enough to keep the number of deaths at a few.

"We've created the umbrella to protect the faeries from lemon juice, if Radella managed to get her hands on some." Agatha sat on a three-legged stool. "We've also made sure to have plenty of strengthening potion on hand, thanks to Gorna. Rachel will stand on one tower with Hanna and make sure her arrows never run out. I'm doing my best to keep Logan at the back of the fight, but the boy is rambunctious and excited, the little fool."

Shayna would think of some way to keep the boy safe. Once the trench was breached, he could not be in harm's way. "Kasdeya will be stationed on one tower and Agatha on another. That gives us a three-point advantage of sight over the field. It sounds as if all the preparation we can do are done. Tomorrow, we rest and feast in preparation. I will be gone with Kasdeya for the rest of the day. She's needs strengthening."

She located Kasdeya at the shooting range. "I'd like you to come with me."

"Okay." She set down her rifle. "Will I need my weapon?"

"Bring your sword, but I have no plans for us to need it." She held out her hand. When Kasdeya placed hers in Shayna's, they teleported to a small country church in the Ozarks.

"Why are we here?" Kasdeya frowned. "We don't have time for a sightseeing trip."

"Inside this building is a group of people who have heard of the plight in New York. They are in prayer before they head to the city to fight. Churches all across this land are full of such brave men and women. I think you need to see what our sacrifice is for." Shayna pushed open the doors and took a seat in the back.

The peace of the church, the soft whispers of prayers, helped to ease her troubled spirit as she hoped it would Kasdeya. A few parishioners sent them friendly glances but returned to their prayers, except for one man in a simple button-up shirt and jeans.

The pastor made his way down the aisle and sat in the pew ahead of them. Turning sideways, he said, "I've seen a photo of you in the paper. I'd know you as the faerie queen even without the crown on your head."

"Yes, I am Shayna, queen of The Glen. My friend is in need of encouragement before a great battle."

"I can give her that. Follow me." He led them from the church to a nearby town. "We have two thousand residents. Small compared to what New York has lost. Our country, our world, is full of innocents such as these." He motioned to where children played on swings and slides. "The reason for your fighting is to prevent what has happened in the Big Apple from happening in places such as this, am I correct?"

"You are."

He stared at Kasdeya. "As we speak, I have friends willing to take up arms and come fight with you. I've asked them to stay in case you fail. Do not fail."

Tears ran down Kasdeya's face. "Your people are willing to lay down their lives for strangers?"

He shrugged. "It's the human way. There is still a lot of good in this world that needs protecting." He took her hands. "What you are doing is a wonderful thing."

"I was once a follower of evil. My mind is not strong enough to resist."

"Oh, but it is. All you need to do is focus on what is good and true. Darkness will flee before you. I must return to my congregation. We will continue to pray for your safety." He smiled at them both, then shoved his hands in his pockets and strolled away whistling.

"That is a man who is not full of worry," Shayna said. "Come." This time they teleported to the city of sprites.

The tiny blue creatures flitted from one task to another, singing a joyful tune. "See? Even they do not worry over what they cannot control."

"That's because all the control is in our hands." Kasdeya shook her head. "They have no need to worry. Brigette said we will win the war."

"It will never be completely over. Evil will still prowl our worlds in search of someone to take up its cause. There will always be a need for warriors of the Light." She knew of Kasdeya's and Marshal's plans to travel the world in search of darkness to destroy. "You will not perish, Kasdeya. If Marshal should fall, you will need to go forward with the plans the two of you made. These worlds need a woman such as you."

"A former demon follower?" Her eyes widened.

"You are no longer that person. Stop looking to the past and focus on the future."

"I'd rather not look past the battle at this point."

"You need more proof that hope still lives?" How much more could she show the woman? Ah. She teleported them to a hospital in Montana. They strolled the maternity ward, peering in rooms and listening to the cries of babies. "This is the future we will maintain. New life, Kasdeya. This is what you will be a part of."

"You sound as if you have no future."

Shayna laughed. "My future lies in The Glen with my people. Yours will be in this world. Alone or with others, you will go on."

22
Kasdeya

Kasdeya held onto Shayna's uplifting words the next day, their last day of peace for however long the battle raged. She led Marshal into a secluded spot, protected by boulders and overlooking the camp. She told him of the things Shayna had shown her. "She believes in me."

"You should believe in yourself." He entwined his fingers with hers. "I'm glad to know you'll go on if I fall."

"You won't fall. I know it in my heart." *Oh, please don't die.*

"Either way, let's not dwell on it. Let's enjoy the time we have." He leaned his head against the rock behind him. "We've a large group of skilled fighters. I'll be fine. I'm not such a weakling, you know." He smiled down at her. "Agatha promised us all a potion. If it's anything like the one I had before the last battle, I'll be invincible."

"Silly man." She leaned her head on his shoulder. "No one is invincible. Will the vampires fight with weapons?"

"They and the demons had swords the last time. There's no time for the vampires to bite and turn anyone. It's kill or be killed. No lie, they're aggressive fighters."

She straightened as a helicopter flew overhead. As she watched, men jumped from the plane and parachuted to the ground. "The SWAT team is here!" She grinned. "I thought they were staying in the city."

"I guess they changed their mind. Look." He pointed at the helicopter's belly. "A water tank. Want to guess what it holds?"

"Another advantage." She jumped to her feet and pulled his hands until he stood. "Let's go welcome them."

Harry Dodge turned as they rushed toward his group of twelve men. "We aren't much, but we're ready to fight."

"Glad to have you." Marshal shook the man's hand. "Does Shayna know?"

"I'm sure Pierce told her. We radioed in yesterday that we were arriving."

"Then, let's get you filled in." Kasdeya led them to Shayna's tent.

"Welcome." Shayna stood from the chair she'd sat in. "Please, refresh yourselves, then see if I've missed anything in my plans."

"That's more for Castion to look at, but it won't hurt for us to know all the details." Dodge removed his helmet. "Since we have riot gear, we'd like to be placed in front of the civilians."

"We've armor," Kasdeya said.

"But we can push them back with our shields." He tapped a finger on the map. We'll stand on this side of the trenches and slow them down by pushing them in. How about silver spikes at the bottom?"

"Good idea." Shayna headed for the tent flap. "I'll get Agatha working on that. It'll be close, but we'll have them ready."

Pierce entered the tent. "I am glad to see you." He clapped Dodge on the shoulder. "It's going to be dangerous."

"And risky."

"Exciting." Pierce grinned.

"Stimulating."

Kasdeya rolled her eyes. Men. "People will die."

"For sure." Dodge flashed her a smile. "My bet is on more of them, though. Now, where is this faerie food I've heard about?"

Pierce laughed. "Follow me. You can eat your fill and then some."

They trooped to the dining tent where tables were loaded down with food. No matter how much she ate, Kasdeya would never tire of food from The Glen. While she ate, she enjoyed the reactions of Dodge and his men as they took their first bite.

Laughter and song rang out as Seamus danced a jig up and down the table, scattering food and plates to applause and good-natured griping. Faeries in multi-colored gowns refilled plates and goblets. Today, they feasted. Tomorrow, they'd fight.

"My friends." Shayna stood at the head of the table. "Eat, drink. Whiskey and water flows. Food is in abundance. Dance and sing songs of rejoicing, for tomorrow we rid the world of a large chunk of evil. We are not from different worlds any longer but one force to be reckoned with."

"Hear, hear!" Voices rose.

She sat to the sound of applause and smiled in Kasdeya's direction, a question in her eyes.

Kasdeya nodded. She was good. She was ready to meet Radella in the designated spot, and she'd fight with all her strength until Shayna arrived. She'd set aside her fear of what might come. Instead, she reached for Marshal's hand.

"Come with me."

"Anywhere." He smiled.

She led him to where they'd sat earlier that morning and took both of his hands in hers. "I pledge to you, here and now, in the way of the faeries. Will you bind to me, Luke Marshal? It's all we have time for until this is over, and we can have a church ceremony." She stared through tears in his eyes.

"I take this vow as seriously as any marriage vow, Kassy. But I still want a ceremony in a church where I put my grandmother's ring on your finger." He lowered his head and claimed her lips in a kiss before leading her further from camp.

Radella

Radella watched from her peak on the mountaintop and sneered at the sounds of singing and laughter that reached her ears. Let them laugh and play. Tomorrow, they'd die and this world would be hers. She'd turn the humans to immortals and then take the fae world as her slaves and feeding objects.

The wind whipped her hair around her head and still she stood there. Loneliness filled her empty heart despite the demons whirling overhead. They were not her friends. They followed her orders out of fear because of the lies she'd told regarding Abaddon's release the next day. If they disobeyed, they feared the consequences more than they feared perishing on the battlefield.

This war would be won because of her! Her strength and brilliance. She'd forged battle plans alone with no counsel. Shayna could not say the same.

Stupid trenches with silver spikes. Her vampires could leap the ditch with ease. Her demons would pluck the mortal fighters from the ground and drop them on the very spikes they thought to kill her followers with. She rubbed her hands together, barely able to control her excitement over the next day.

"I'm coming, Shayna!" She raised her arms to the sky and screamed.

Shayna

The table quieted as Radella's challenge rang out. Mouths full of food stilled in chewing. Seamus stopped dancing. Sprites stopped darting. All turned to stare at Shayna.

She forced an expression of nonchalance. "We know she's there. Let her crow."

Nervous laughter floated around the room. Catcalls rang out when Kasdeya and Marshal rushed into the tent. Only a fool couldn't see what they'd been doing. Shayna was happy for them. Perhaps, they'd wed in the very church she'd taken Kasdeya to the day before.

"Everyone, please return to what you were doing. Radella won't do anything today."

"Are you sure?" Pierce leaned close and whispered.

"Of course not," she answered, keeping her voice low. "I intend to slip out in a few minutes to make sure she doesn't try to sabotage anything. I do believe Brigette would have known if I was to face her today instead of tomorrow."

"Brigette saw things, but things change with the choices we make. What she saw is not a sure thing."

Shayna tossed down her napkin. "Then I will patrol the area now."

"I'll come with you."

Irritated, a feeling she rarely had, she nodded and strode from the tent. Outside, she took a deep breath of the cool mountain air and stared at the myriad of stars against an inky sky. A sky darker than normal because of the waiting evil.

She'd like nothing more than to confront Radella at that moment and stop the battle from happening, but the vampire had something up her leather sleeve and it wouldn't happen until morning. Yet… "I smell a stench on the air. You might as well step out, Radella."

"No, thank you. What's with the crown? Parading around, are you?"

Shayna motioned for Pierce to be alert and scout around outside the tents.

"Call it a morale booster." She peered around the tent's corner.

An icy wind blasted her in the face. The sky overhead whirled in a circle. Shayna froze, trying to determine what trick Radella played. The night filled with the sharp sound of demons shrieking.

"How's that for a morale booster?" Radella called. "They can do that all night."

Olga rose from where she slept and reached up, grabbing a demon in her hand. She squeezed, raining ash upon Shayna's head. "Stupid woman. She'll regret disturbing my slumber." She plucked another from the sky. "I, too, can do this all night."

"No need." Agatha emerged from the tent and cast a spell that shut out all sound outside the shield. "There. Eight hours of blessed silence." Wrapping her cloak around her, she ducked into a smaller tent and turned off the lantern.

Shayna laughed. Enjoy your rest, old friend. What would they do without her?

"She reminds me of my grandmother," Castion said, joining her outside.

"Your grandmother was a witch?"

"She could be, when I was bad." His teeth flashed. "No, I mean her sass. I'm glad she's on our side."

"Me, too." Although it had taken some convincing when they'd first met. Agatha, thinking she was the last of her kind, had wanted to be left alone to live her life in whatever manner she wanted with the time she had left. Instead, she'd fight in a war tomorrow, something no old woman should have to do.

"Come on." Pierce took her hand. "You need rest as much as the others."

"One more patrol around. Will you come with me?"

"Yes."

Together, they strolled the perimeter of the shield. Shayna listened to the quiet murmurs and snores of the others as they slept or prepared to. Her people. She'd never been so proud of anything in her life.

They rounded a corner and came face-to-face with Radella. The vampire sneered from the other side of the shield, her palm flat against the barrier she couldn't cross. With her other hand, she made a slicing motion across her throat.

Tricks of intimidation wouldn't work on Shayna. She smiled and wiggled her fingers in a wave before continuing on her way. "I can rest easy knowing nothing can get through until the shield lifts. We'll be ready an hour before then."

Pierce followed her into their tent. "In case there's no time tomorrow, remember I love you, and I can't think of a better person to lead this group of mismatched warriors. You took people from all races and turned them into something to be feared. You truly are a queen."

She stepped into his arms. "I couldn't do it without you. Thank you for believing me that first day."

"Well, it involved you taking off your shirt and knocking me on my ass, but I believed after that. Thank goodness these other humans didn't take as much convincing."

Her laugh muffled against his chest. "They had proof enough with all the vampires and demons running around."

"And you didn't have to remove any clothing to show your wings."

"Exactly." She stepped back and peeled off her jacket. "I'm so ready to return to The Glen and stay there for a good long while."

He sobered. "I'd hoped to have a replacement chief of police by now, but I'll still put in my resignation and rule your world at your side. I'm growing tired of violence." He sat on the edge of the cot. "I'd thought maybe Marshal would take my place, but I think he and Kasdeya have other plans."

"Yes, they plan on saving the world."

23

Kasdeya

$\mathcal{A}$ somber group of people took their positions on the field. The dragons rested off to the side, prepared to take flight at the first glimpse of the enemy and wipe out as many as they could before reaching the camp.

Kasdeya stepped reluctantly from Marshal's arms and cupped his cheek. "I love you."

"I love you, too. Come back to me, Kassy." His voice broke.

"I'll be back before you know I'm gone." She forced a smile and failed, her chin quivering. "Once Shayna shows, I'll climb that tower and focus on keeping you safe."

"Concentrate on keeping yourself safe."

A trumpet sounded.

Kasdeya glanced at the field. A swarm of darkness headed toward them, dark and menacing like a desert haboob. A tidal wave of vampires and demons sprinted and flew in their direction. She swallowed back the bile rising in her throat. She wasn't a warrior; she was nothing more than a human trying to right the many wrongs she'd done.

Shayna waved a hand in her direction, telling her it was time to go. Slinging her rifle over her shoulder, Kasdeya took off at a run to where they'd agreed she would lure Radella. Not wanting to change her mind, she didn't look back although she could feel Marshal's... Luke's eyes on her. She'd need to get used to calling him Luke since she was now Mrs. Marshal. She grinned and ducked behind a bush that offered little protection from anyone actually looking for her.

She rubbed her hands together against the cold breeze blowing across the mountaintop. The sun began its ascent, kissing the peak with a touch of gold. Too bad the stories of vampires being allergic to the sun no longer held true. She'd relish watching Radella bake under its rays.

"You came."

She whirled to face a grinning, fang-bared vampire. The wind blew her dark hair away from her face. Terrifyingly beautiful, her dead eyes focused on Kasdeya.

"Of course." She sprang to her feet. "I'm looking forward to your final descent to hell." Her lungs squeezed, her breath escaping in a wheeze.

"Isn't it wonderful to be human again with all its pain and heartache?" Radella's grin widened.

Kasdeya dug in her pocket for her inhaler.

"Wonderful. May I?"

The vampire shrugged. "Of course. I wouldn't want an unfair advantage, after all. You're number one on my list. I still have a queen to slay. If it's any consolation, when I get to your man, I'll take my time."

Kasdeya raised her inhaler to her mouth, squeezed, and inhaled before taking a firm hold of her sword again. Of all the times for her asthma to attack. "I'm ready."

"To defend your queen? Your man? Your world?" Radella laughed. "None of which is worth saving."

"Is this the queen you want to kill?" Shayna leaped into the air, coming down on bare ground as Radella spun out of the way.

While the vampire's attention was on Shayna, Kasdeya raced for the battlefield and took her position on one of the towers. Already the battle raged as demons flew over the trenches and dove for those on the towers. One sank its claws into a faerie archer, dropping the man onto the spikes in the ditch. *Smart move, Radella.* Kasdeya took aim and blasted the demon from the sky.

Several of the vampires had already jumped the trench, while others placed planks of wood in a makeshift bridge. Gorna and the other dragons rained fire on the heads of the demons. With Alvar's newer breed, fire only seemed to make them stronger.

The SWAT helicopter hovered overhead, its

propellers thumping, and dumped its load of holy water. The shrieks of slayed demons joined the battle cries.

Pierce yelled something to Gorna, changing the dragon's direction. Now, instead of breathing fire, they clutched demons in their hands and dropped them into the trench where a second helicopter had dumped another load of water. Steam rose as demons fell.

A horde of the evil things surrounded a smaller dragon, forcing it to the ground under their weight. Kasdeya picked off as many of them as she could in hopes of saving the creature whose emerald scales shone in the morning light. To her right, Hanna fired arrow after arrow at the vampires crossing the bridge.

Below, her brother weaved his way between the fighters to reach the front line where the SWAT team created a barrier of strong men holding riot shields. As one, they moved forward driving back the enemy. While they sent many into the trench, still more circled around coming in at the sides.

Shayna needed to be quick. The enemy was getting the upper hand, fast.

"Luke, get Logan!" Kasdeya pointed at the boy who had become the target of a large male undead.

Luke gave her a thumbs-up and sprinted for the boy. With her heart in her throat, Kasdeya watched as he yanked the teenager out of the clutches of the enemy and plunged his sword into the vampire's heart. As a fresh group surrounded them, Luke thrust Logan behind him.

The very thing Shayna warned them about had

happened. The enemy had managed to separate the fighters for the Light. Each group faced more undead than they could fight. Kasdeya laid down her rifle and descended the ladder as the tower holding the witches collapsed under the weight of more than a handful of demons.

Shayna

"Listen to the screams." Radella circled around Shayna. "That's the sound of your people dying while you dance with me." She pretended to glance at a watch on her wrist that didn't exist. "Haven't we played long enough?"

Shayna had lost track of the time the two had fought. Her sword arm grew heavy. She'd let her people down. The magical crown on her head kept her from succumbing to the many bites Radella had inflicted but did nothing to keep up her endurance. This had to end. Now. She needed to do something drastic.

She lowered her sword. "You win."

"What?" Radella stopped, blinking. "You're giving up?"

"Yes. I'm weary."

"You lie." She narrowed her eyes.

Shayna shrugged and knelt, leaning her head to the side. With her left hand, she reached up and removed the crown.

Radella laughed. "If only your people could see

you now." She moved closer, fangs bared.

When she stepped within reach, Shayna withdrew the dagger in her right hand and lunged to her feet. The vampire was fast. She leaped back, tripping over a pile of rocks and dropping out of sight off a small cliff.

Shayna followed, jumping over the ledge and landing on her feet. She straddled Radella, one hand clutching the knife. "I take great pleasure in this, but there are winners and losers in a battle, and I will not lose." She dropped the crown and clutched the jeweled handle in both hands. With all her strength, she plunged the blade into Radella's heart.

The vampire howled in agony before turning to ash and blowing away on the wind. Without taking time to relish in the deed, Shayna placed the crown back on her head and raced to the battlefield.

The demons and undead fell where they'd flown or stood. Those of Shayna's people left standing went among the fallen and finished them off.

"You did it." Pierce glanced over his shoulder. "You look a bit worse for wear, though. You all right?"

She nodded. "No one looks unscathed."

"It was a bloody one for sure. I started to think Radella had bested you."

"In a way, she did." She studied the field for signs of her friends. Her gaze darted from one fallen warrior to another, her heart sinking more and more as she failed to find the ones she looked for. They couldn't all be gone. It wasn't possible. She whirled at movement behind her.

Luke, supported by Kasdeya, stepped from

behind a tent. The man's arm hung useless at his side.

"It took you long enough," Kasdeya said. "You should have let me stay to help."

"If you'd have stayed there, darling, I'd be dead." Luke sagged onto a crate. "You saved mine and Logan's lives. Where is the boy?"

Not just him, but so many others were missing. Shayna climbed the one tower still standing. The sun sat high overhead, illuminating the field littered with bodies. Movement. There. She peered down to see Castion, his face almost unrecognizable under the blood, stagger to his feet. Slowly more came out of hiding or got to their feet from where they'd collapsed, most unsteady under the weight of their injuries.

Shayna climbed back down the ladder. Time to sort the living from the dead. She'd have to keep her emotions at bay until the task was done, and she knew how big her failure was to her people.

Kasdeya

"I'm leaving you in Nurse Ida's capable hands," Kasdeya told Luke. "I need to help Shayna find other survivors."

"I understand." He kissed her hand and let her go.

She stepped from the tent and headed to the right where Shayna stared at a lifeless Earin. Tears ran down her face. Lying next to him, her hand stretched out as if to take his, was Becky.

"How many?" Kasdeya asked. "Deema? Agatha?"

"I haven't found them." Shayna swiped the back of her hand across her face.

"I will search with you."

Shayna nodded. "Where did you last see the witches?"

"When their tower fell."

They headed in that direction. Kasdeya's heart fell. Logan and Hanna knelt beside their mother, her neck at a weird angle. There was no sight of Agatha or the others. The kids didn't look up when they approached. Instead, they lifted Rachel into their arms and carried her to the tent designated for bodies.

Grumblings came from under a nearby collapsed canvas tent. Shayna pulled at the cloth and helped a disgruntled Agatha to her feet. "I feared the worst, my old friend." She wrapped her in a hug.

"I'm not that easy to kill. Easy on the hug. Every inch of me hurts." Agatha pulled back and dusted off her robes. "How bad is it?"

"We've lost Earin, Rachel, and Becky. I'm still searching for more."

Agatha collapsed to the ground. "Leave me here to mourn my friend for a few minutes. I'll help you search in a bit." She covered her face with her hands.

"I hope she isn't again the last of her kind," Shayna said as they moved away.

"She seems indestructible, doesn't she?" Kasdeya looked back to see Agatha's shoulders shaking.

"She isn't, though. A part of her is breaking now." Shayna lifted boards of the fallen tower and tossed them aside to reveal the other witches, wounded, broken, but alive. Together, she and Kasdeya helped them to sitting positions.

"Help will come for you. Stay put," Shayna said.

"Look." Kasdeya pointed to where Deema made her way slowly in their direction.

With a cry of joy, Shayna dashed to her friend, Kasdeya following close behind. "I was so afraid." Shayna wrapped her in a hug. "Payson?"

"I haven't found him." Deema sagged in her arms. "The last I saw of him, he was with the SWAT team. I fear they've all fallen." Her shoulders shook with sobs.

"There is hope until we lay eyes on a body."

Deema raised red-rimmed eyes. "We lost so many."

"Radella was stronger than I'd thought she could be. Alvar's magic coursing through her veins almost changed the course of this war."

"All right, you two. There's time for mourning later. Let's find this man of yours." Kasdeya's tears joined theirs, not because of sorrow, but because her man lived and breathed. She hoped the same of Payson.

"None of this is your fault," Deema said, pulling away from Shayna. "You fought bravely or you would not be standing here. We could have lost everyone, but we haven't." She motioned to the field where more and more of their fighters were getting to their feet. "Clark!" She hobbled toward Payson, who hurried toward her.

"Do you want to rest?" Kasdeya peered into Shayna's weary face. "You're injured. You kind of resemble a pin cushion for vampire teeth." She tried to smile and lessen the burden weighing down on the faerie.

"Not yet. I cannot until I have seen all of the living and stared into each face of those I failed."

"Deema is right. You fought hard for these warriors. Because of you, the world is not overcome by darkness." She turned Shayna to face her. "Because of you I'm saved, our men our safe, those children…the people of that church. You saved us all, Shayna, knowing you could have perished, yet you faced evil and conquered it.."

She shook her head. "Brigette said I would not die."

"She is not a sorceress. She could have been wrong." Kasdeya stepped back and crossed her arms. "Enough pity. You're the queen. Step up and act like one. These poor people are casualties of war. It could have been a lot worse." She took another step back in case she'd angered the faerie enough for her to retaliate.

"You're right. Abaddon is in chains. He has no followers here." She met Kasdeya's glare. "But there will be others in time to take his and Radella's place."

"Then we'll deal with them then. Are you done feeling sorry for yourself?"

Shayna chuckled. "You are a remarkable woman." She clapped a hand on Kasdeya's shoulder. "I am proud to have you on my side."

By the time night fell, more than half of their numbers still breathed. The hospital tent was filled with the injured, another with the dead. Among the lost were all but two of the SWAT team, them being the first line of defense, fewer than half of the mercenaries, Earin, Rachel, and Becky, and more faeries than Kasdeya could count. Despite the sun's brilliance overhead, it was a dark day indeed.

She and Shayna stood next to Gorna who stared down at the poor dragon who'd been overcome by demons.

"She will not live," Shayna said. "We are having Abaddon brought here so you can exact your revenge."

"What is Gorna going to do?" Revenge tasted less sweet after the bloodbath she'd witnessed that morning.

"Feed him to the dying one. For a dragon to eat one filled with such evil as Abaddon would mean death." Shayna knelt and placed a hand on the green dragon's neck. "But since she is already dying, we can accomplish it without further damage. It will lessen her suffering by hastening the outcome."

Kasdeya turned as a shackled Abaddon was dragged toward them. "I'm not sure I have the stomach for this after all."

"The Light has overcome. This is the only way to vanquish his evil. The fires of hell will not consume him. He cannot be killed by mortal weapons. Stand well back," Shayna said. "You must not be caught in the blast. Rise, my dying friend, and enter into the hereafter."

Shayna grabbed the end of Abaddon's chain as the dragon fought to stand. She hooked the end to a large boulder and stepped back.

Despite the urge to look away, Kasdeya couldn't. She'd waited a long time for this.

Abaddon struggled against his chains, cursing and begging for his life. Why did those who thought life held little value fight to live when their time came to die?

The dragon leaned over him and took him into her mouth. Her throat convulsed as she swallowed. Seconds later, the dragon exploded in a shower of flickering sparks. It was done.

Kasdeya turned and vomited.

24

Kasdeya

Shayna had allowed the injured to recuperate in The Glen. With the medical skills of the faerie nurses, recovery took less time than in the human world. Rather than their usual jeweled-colored clothing, every fae wore a shade of gray as they mourned those who wouldn't return.

Kasdeya reclined on large pillows in the throne room with those left from their core group. She nestled in the curve of Luke's healed broken arm and dwelled on how blessed she was. Life would go on, here and in her world because of the sacrifices of these people.

"You two still plan on combing the world for evildoers?" Castion, a patch over his missing eye, asked.

"Yes." Kasdeya glanced at Luke, then back to Castion. "We feel it's our purpose. Why?"

"Me and my men want to be a part of it. We've never fought for something so honorable before, nor have we ever fought with such brave people. It seems a shame to go back to our old ways, although the money was nice."

Kasdeya laughed. "I'll pay you, and we'd love to have you tag along. Come see the world with us and be a hero."

"You're having a baby?" Agatha shrieked where she stood in front of Shayna seated on her throne.

Shayna put a finger to her lips. "You are horrible at keeping secrets."

"You fought in a battle while carrying a child?" Agatha shook her head. "I've met crazy before, but you're queen of that, too."

"I couldn't stop what needed doing," Shayna said. "That's why I said nothing."

Pierce scoffed. "We've already discussed this. My wife is unrepentant." His gaze softened as he turned his head in her direction.

Kasdeya would have done the same in her shoes. The war had to be fought in order to bring a child into a better place.

Shayna stood. "Come. We've a wedding to attend." She smiled at Kasdeya and Luke. "The bride must get ready." She held out her hand.

Kasdeya placed hers into the queen's and let herself be led to the queen's chambers. On the bed lay a gown of such a bright white it hurt her eyes. She ran her hand over a fabric so soft it was like feeling nothing at all. "It's the most beautiful thing I've ever seen." She glanced down at her red leather. "I'll be glad to get out of these clothes I've worn for so long. I started to think they were a part of me."

"They are. A part of you that no longer exists." Shayna pointed her shaft at Kasdeya, melting the red away and leaving a yellow one in its place. "You are now filled with sunshine, Cassandra Brown. Although, you can wear whatever you want, whenever you want, but when you visit The Glen, you will be as bright as a daffodil."

Shayna draped the wedding gown over her arm and teleported them to a room in the back of the small country church. From the voices coming from the sanctuary, their friends had arrived first.

Kasdeya's heart rate increased. She'd pledged to Luke, already joined as man and wife, but now she'd do so in the time-honored tradition of making vows before God. "I can't believe I haven't been struck by lightning for stepping foot in a house of God."

"Forgiveness and second chances," Shayna said, changing to a gown of brilliant blue. "I'm honored to be the one to hand you into the capable hands of your husband. You've given me a great gift."

"No greater than the one of acceptance you showed me." Kasdeya changed into the gown that flowed over her body like liquid silk. On her head, she wore a wreath of tiny white roses.

The double doors opened.

Blue sprites darted around her and Shayna as they marched down the aisle, singing a sweet melody that brought tears to Kasdeya's eyes. Despite all the bad, she almost relished her bad. Without it, she wouldn't be here, with these people, walking down the aisle to the man who loved her with all his heart.

Deema stood in front of the altar as maid of honor, no longer in gray, but wearing a gown of deep purple. Across from her smiled Payson who stood next to Pierce.

Shayna placed her hand in Marshal's, smiled up at the pastor, and took her place next to Deema.

The pastor laughed. "I have never had the privilege of performing a wedding like this before. What an honor! Dearly beloved…"

The next morning, Kasdeya stood in the airport with Marshal, Castion, and his men. In the pack she carried on her back was Agatha's crystal ball. The witch said it would tell them where to go, and so they headed to Ireland to help finish what Seamus had cut down. After that, who knew? Only the ball could tell.

Since she'd bought an airplane, and one of Castion's men was an accomplished pilot, they carried crates of weapons, holy water, and silver into the cabin. Kasdeya had wanted Agatha to accompany them, but the old woman refused to leave Shayna. So, they had a witch with them named Lucille, a petite, black-haired woman with the energy of a hummingbird and the cheerfulness of a sprite.

"Ready to kick some darkness ass?" Marshal asked, putting his arm around her shoulder.

"More than ready." She smiled up at him. "It's great to have a purpose."

"It sure is." He lowered his head and kissed her as the sun rose, casting its rays through the cabin window.

The End

Dear Reader,

It's kind of sad when you say goodbye to characters you've spent so much time with, and Shayna, Deema, Kasdeya, and three handsome, honorable detectives are no different. Let's not forget the feisty witch, Agatha. While these stories are an allegory of a sort about the epic battle of good vs. evil, I never once intended to show anything but God's love within these pages. Go in the Light, my friends, and may you meet someone pure of heart enough to change your world.

Cynthia

Website at www.cynthiahickey.com

Multi-published and Amazon and ECPA Best-Selling author Cynthia Hickey has sold close to a million copies of her works since 2013. She has taught a Continuing Education class at the 2015 American Christian Fiction Writers conference, several small ACFW chapters and RWA chapters. She and her husband run the small press, Winged Publications, which includes some of the CBA's best well-known authors. She lives in Arizona with her husband, one of their seven children, two dogs, one cat, and three box turtles. She has nine grandchildren who keep her busy and tell everyone they know that "Nana is a writer".

Shayna, book one. Get it here
Connect with me on FaceBook
Twitter
Bookbub
Sign up for my newsletter and receive a free short story
www.cynthiahickey.com

Follow me on Amazon

Enjoy other books by Cynthia Hickey

Fantasy
Fate of the Faes
Shayna
Deema

Time Travel
The Portal

A Hollywood Murder
Killer Pose, book 1
Killer Snapshot, book 2
Shoot to Kill, book 3

Shady Acres Mysteries
Beware the Orchids, book 1
Path to Nowhere
Poison Foliage
Poinsettia Madness
Deadly Greenhouse Gases
Vine Entrapment

CLEAN BUT GRITTY

Highland Springs

Murder Live
Say Bye to Mommy
To Breathe Again

Colors of Evil Series

Shades of Crimson
Coral Shadows

The Pretty Must Die Series

Ripped in Red, book 1
Pierced in Pink, book 2
Wounded in White, book 3
Worthy, The Complete Story

Lisa Paxton Mystery Series

Eenie Meenie Miny Mo
Jack Be Nimble
Hickory Dickory Dock

One Hour (A short story thriller)

INSPIRATIONAL
(scroll down to see clean books without inspirational
message)

Whisper Sweet Nothings (a short romance)

Nosy Neighbor Series
Anything For A Mystery, Book 1
A Killer Plot, Book 2
Skin Care Can Be Murder, Book 3
Death By Baking, Book 4
Jogging Is Bad For Your Health, Book 5
Poison Bubbles, Book 6
A Good Party Can Kill You, Book 7 (Final)
Nosy Neighbor collection

Christmas with Stormi Nelson

The Summer Meadows Series
Fudge-Laced Felonies, Book 1
Candy-Coated Secrets, Book 2
Chocolate-Covered Crime, Book 3
Maui Macadamia Madness, Book 4
All four novels in one collection

The River Valley Mystery Series
Deadly Neighbors, Book 1
Advance Notice, Book 2
The Librarian's Last Chapter, Book 3
All three novels in one collection

Historical cozy
Hazel's Quest

Historical Romances
Runaway Sue
Taming the Sheriff
Sweet Apple Blossom

Finding Love the Harvey Girl Way
Cooking With Love
Guiding With Love
Serving With Love
Warring With Love
All 4 in 1

A Wild Horse Pass Novel
They Call Her Mrs. Sheriff, book 1 (A Western Romance)

Finding Love in Disaster
The Rancher's Dilemma
The Teacher's Rescue
The Soldier's Redemption

Woman of courage Series

A Love For Delicious
Ruth's Redemption
Charity's Gold Rush
Mountain Redemption
Woman of Courage series (all four books)

Short Story Westerns
Desert Rose
Desert Lilly
Desert Belle
Desert Daisy
Flowers of the Desert 4 in 1

Romantic Suspense

Overcoming Evil series
Mistaken Assassin
Captured Innocence
Mountain of Fear
Exposure at Sea
A Secret to Die for
Collision Course
Romantic Suspense of 5 books in 1

The Game
Suspicious Minds

Contemporary

Romance in Paradise
Maui Magic
Sunset Kisses
Deep Sea Love
3 in 1

Finding a Way Home

Service of Love

Christmas

Handcarved Christmas
The Payback Bride
Curtain Calls and Christmas Wishes
Christmas Gold
A Christmas Stamp
Snowflake Kisses

The Red Hat's Club (Contemporary novellas)

Finally
Suddenly
Surprisingly
The Red Hat's Club 3 – in 1

Short Story

One Hour (A short story thriller)
Whisper Sweet Nothings (a Valentine short romance)

www.ingramcontent.com/pod-product-compliance
Lightning Source LLC
Chambersburg PA
CBHW061031120726
47910CB00006B/2196